The Open End:

The Open End:

Short Stories

by

Rhett W. Whitaker

SCRIBBLING
— B O O K S —

For Kelsey

Words will never suffice.

Please keep an open mind:

Round and Round

You forget what it feels like, the sun on your face and the rest of the world awake, alive and buzzing. Bob didn't miss it too much; he'd always been a night owl, so the switch to the graveyard shift had been easier for him than for most other drivers. Besides, he told himself, it's a hell of a lot easier to maneuver a bus when the streets are empty. The extra pay didn't hurt, either.

Things were always desolate early in the shift, with only a few stumbling bar flies making their wobbly way home together; that night was no different. He passed a pair of them and slowed to see if they needed a lift, but they gave no indication that they had seen him or cared. He applied gentle pressure to the gas pedal, and the bus gathered itself once again down the lonely city street.

A light drizzle left thousands of little prisms on the windshield, halos which swelled and burst as the bus juggernauted onward under the streetlights. Bob flipped a switch, and the wiper blades went about the business of slowly smearing the world. Through the side windows, he could still see the red brick buildings of downtown flashing by, the occasional office-window puppet show starring some insomniac work-aholic. Realtors peered in at him from bus stop benches, empty eyes and empty smiles gleaming white next to empty promises of fulfilling the American Dream. "No Credit? No Problem!" they screamed in comic sans. Bob begged to differ.

His shift rolled on, with a handful of motley passengers taking up residence in the bus just long enough to reach the places they needed to be at that questionable hour. It was an odd night that passed without at least one of these transitory denizens striking up a conversation with Bob; on bad nights, the conversation would be dull, unintelligible, or end with a steaming font of self-control issues coming his way. On good nights, there was a chance that the passenger had a story to tell, one that was interesting without Bob having to try. Some people were genuinely unique and honestly offbeat: one woman had wound up in the country as a mail order bride, only to flee her marital home as soon as her citizenship was established. Her husband had been kind to her, she admitted, but her aim had always been to escape the rampant oppression of her home country. Kind or not, her husband was not the man she would have chosen, and if she were going to live a life of freedom, damn it, she was going to do it right. Another passenger explained at length how he had loved his cousin in the wrong way, and how adding incest to being a fag was not going to fly. Not where he was from, in any case. He'd come here to clear his mind and get a fresh start. That, and he'd heard that the art scene wasn't bad.

These were the stories that drove Bob. Unfortunately, they were drying up more quickly than usual that night; the last twenty-five minutes before his state-mandated break were spent with slothful windshield wipers as his only company.

He pulled his behemoth into the depot just before he was slated to go off the clock. He preferred to take his breaks in the bus, as none of the three guys who took turns manning dispatch at this time of night were known for their conversationalism, and all had such heinous B.O. that Bob had to mouthbreathe any time he was forced to talk to any of them for longer than it took for the standard pleasantries. He turned the bus into the second row and found a spot as close to the building as he could. When things were this shitty and wet out, it was nice not to have to walk so far to get to the head.

Bob shook his jacket hood as he lowered it, showering water onto the mat at the reception entrance and sprinkling a few drops into his crop of ashen hair as the door swung shut behind him. He'd planned on four minutes for the trip: two to piss and wash his face, one to grab something from vending, and one to check the schedule for any changes to his route. He was three and a half minutes through the plan when he was accosted by Gary, the Stooge who was on duty that night. Bob's mouth grew dry as Gary regaled him with the tale of the Wicked Tacos He Ate Last Night; Bob excused himself by saying he needed to make a phone call. Despite the late hour, Gary did not appear to suspect any chicanery.

Bob's return to the outside world was greeted by receding rain, which had cleared almost completely by the time he made it back to the bus. He couldn't have said what made him pull his hand back when he reached to open the bus door, but the urge was insistent. He decided to spend the rest of his break stretching his legs in the adjacent neighborhood. It was supposed to be up-and-coming, and he was curious as to why people were so worked up about it.

After a few blocks of freshly renovated apartments, a right turn took him into one of the patches in the area that had missed the most recent wave of investment. Outcroppings of boarded up storefronts muscled in between the shops that were still making a fight of it. Bob looked up at a shuttered Indian market called *Butt Sweet & Food* and tried to figure things out. His train of thought was broken by a swath of motion in the alley next to the store; closer inspection revealed a man who seemed to be wrestling with a sheet of corrugated plastic and slipping around in a puddle of cardboard swill. Bob hustled over to offer his assistance.

"Brother, you don't know how much I appreciate it," the other man exhaled, his face falling out of traction. "I almost had this thing set up when it started raining, and now it's all gone to shit. I spent a week collecting this stuff."

Bob helped the man make the best of the situation. In the end, the best turned out not to be very good at all. The homeless-again man stood there holding his head to keep it from shaking; Bob asked if he'd like to hang out in the bus and warm up while he cleared his mind.

"You're seriously making me wonder where you came from," the man said. "Yes, thanks. That'd be great."

The two hurried back to the depot, with the rain making an unwelcome comeback just as they turned the final corner. Bob asked that the man wait at the depot gate, as he wasn't exactly sure of company policy when it came to helping people out. A few minutes later, the bus came rumbling up, the boom lifted, and the man climbed aboard; Bob motioned to the seats behind him and invited his guest to make himself at home. The man took a seat behind Bob and offered his hand, which Bob shook at an odd angle. "Thanks again. Name's Hal, by the way," the man said. Bob introduced himself and asked if Hal wanted to stay on for the rest of the shift. "Nowhere else to go, especially not in this rain," Hal said, squinting through the windshield. "As long as I'm not putting you out." Bob indicated that it was no trouble and confided that he didn't have anyone waiting for him either, apart from his pet parakeet, with whom he was not on speaking terms at the moment. Pumpkin knew what she'd done.

The second half of the shift produced few passengers, which allowed the two men to get to know each other better. Hal asked Bob how he liked his job and talked at length about his hometown; it had been better than five years since he'd been back there. When Bob didn't ask, Hal offered to tell him how he'd wound up on the street. Bob left it up to Hal, insisting that such things weren't any of his business and that he didn't want to pry. "Bullshit," replied Hal. "I bet you're dying to know. Everyone's dying to know." The story was more mundane than Bob had expected, which in turn was fairly shocking. It made Bob worry about his own prospects; he resolved to check over his retirement plan the next chance he got.

"The bitch of it is, you're so busy trying to scrape enough together to get you through the day that you don't have any time or energy left to work on finding a way out," Hal said after Bob had returned from the mini-mart, bag of chips and bottled water in hand. "Going to the shelter is nice in theory, but they can't really help you, either. Not when the place is so packed all the time. They try their best, but they're just barely making ends meet as it is. Panhandling is the go-to during the day when people are out, but the best thing you can do to get some cash—best *legal* thing you can do, I gotta draw the line somewhere—best thing you can do is collect bottles and cans during your down hours. You get some looks when you go to recycle them, but those things add up, believe me. One of those," he said, standing up to point out the window at a squat concrete trashcan with a half dome lid, "probably has at least fifty cents' worth in it."

Bob braked hard to avoid a bicyclist who had run a red light, propelling Hal a few shuffling steps forward into the driver's area. Hal reached for the railing to steady himself, but found that Bob was already restraining him with the back of an outstretched arm. His eyes locked on the road, Bob indicated that such things were not an uncommon occurrence and advised that Hal take a seat. Hal walked, bent-kneed and backward, over to the safe side of the line and sat before picking up where he had left off.

"Sometimes people give you folding money, which is better because it's not so heavy. It's easier to spend, too—nobody wants to be the guy counting out two hundred pennies at the register. It's pretty rare to get anything bigger than a fiver, and even then it's almost not worth it. You wouldn't believe how many self-righteous assholes have lectured me about what I was supposed to do with the ten bucks they were about to give me. They treat you like you're a child or some kind of retard—they assume you fucked your life up somehow and that you need instructions on how to invest the pittance they pull out of their designer wallets. Sure, some of the fault is probably your own, but most folks on the street are just victims of circumstance." He took another gulp from the water bottle and dabbed his mouth with the back of his hand. "There was one guy in the last two years, one, who made me feel like I was still a normal person. Apart from you, brother—this is nice right now. I mean, there are some people who try to be nice, but there's always that pity in their eyes. Their face just says they feel sorry for you, which also means they feel like they're better than you. There's nothing worse for your self-esteem than charity. It's fucked up, but that's just how it is. Anyway, this guy comes up to me, and I wasn't even asking at the time, but he comes up to me, looks me in the eyes, and reaches out to shake my hand. He claps me on the shoulder with his other hand, tells me, 'Things will get better,' and gives me a firm shake. Most of the time people pull away too soon, you know? Like they don't want whatever germs you got. So, he shakes my hand and then runs off to catch a taxi, leaves me standing there with a hundred dollar bill in my hand. I swear to god, I just stood there staring after him as he drove off. He even gave me a little salute from the window." Hal imitated the gesture, putting two fingers up to his forehead and quickly flicking them away. "I didn't even have time to thank the guy. Thing is, I don't think he needed me to. Would you believe that that hundred bucks lasted almost a week, even sharing it out with the other folks?" Hal must have seen the look of confusion on Bob's face in the rearview mirror, because he immediately added, "Oh, you don't keep cash like that to yourself out here. Once you know what it's like to be down, it makes it hard to be greedy."

Bob declined Hal's offer of the last few chips, insisting that he'd already eaten and that the man should enjoy them. Hal checked with Bob again before he dug around in the bottom of the bag, producing two misshapen stragglers which he ate in three bites apiece.

"The folks at the shelter got me an interview lined up next week for a job at the post office," Hal continued after he'd finished sucking the flecks of salt and oil from his fingers. "I'm not sure how I feel about it. On the one hand, it's work and a chance to start again. On the other, if I take the job, it's like I'm accepting that I've fallen this far, and I'm going to be responsible for whatever happens to me from now on." Hal looked at Bob, whose eyes remained on the road. "See, this is great. I never have anyone to bounce this kind of shit off. Saying it out loud makes the right choice pretty obvious. I just need to make sure I get up early enough—they want me there at nine, and I haven't been up before ten in a couple weeks. I really wish I had a suit for this thing. I saw one that looked pretty good at the thrift shop the other day, but they wanted twenty-five bucks for it. Little too rich for my blood these days."

A half block's worth of silence later, Bob contorted himself in his overstuffed seat to retrieve his wallet from his front left pocket. He pulled out a fifty dollar bill, which he held over his right shoulder as he explained to Hal that no one should have to settle for a pretty good suit.

"Listen, I don't want you to think I was fishing before when I mentioned the suit—I was just making conversation. Having some decent company has been more than enough, brother. I'll get by fine," Hal said, bowing slightly as he showed his palms to the back of Bob's head. The bus driver's insistence bore fruit in the end. "Tell you what," Hal relented, "I'll take it, but only if you promise to let me treat you to a steak dinner when I get back on my feet. Deal?" Bob promised and arched his back a little to press the seed money securely into Hal's palm.

Before returning to the depot, Bob took a detour past Hal's attempt at an abode. The men wished each other well, and Hal hopped down onto the still-damp asphalt. He gave Bob a wave through the glass and then turned to survey the destruction the rain had wrought.

Bob didn't see Hal again after that, though not for lack of looking. He thought he'd heard his voice one time while walking through a mall food court, and thought he'd seen him once at a gas station, but the voice had belonged to a man much older than Hal, and the gentleman at the Gas-N-Go had assured Bob that he was just passing through on his way to visit his sister. Bob liked to imagine that Hal was too busy to come around because he had turned down the post office job for a better offer.

One night, months later, Bob found himself negotiating the bus past one of that week's sidewalk crime scenes. As he crawled along behind a rusted out Volvo, he could just make out a man in an ill-fitting herringbone suit lying face-down and motionless on the unfortunate side of the police tape. The officer stepping over the man did not seem to be in any hurry. Bob scolded himself for rubbernecking and got his eyes back on the road.

The Disagreement

Upstairs, shoes are kicked off, thumping. The bedroom door closes.

"That's not what I said."

"You said I hate men. I heard the words come out of your mouth."

"I never said, 'You hate men.' Does that sound like something I would ever say? You know how much I dislike hyperbole."

"Well, then, what did you say?"

"I said that you have a predisposition against men."

Wallet leather slaps on a glass table top. A necklace tinkles as it swings to a stop on a jewelry stand hook.

"You're infuriating, do you know that? You're raking me over the coals for a distinction without a difference."

"And you're not being exacting enough. Of course there's a difference. 'Hate' implies animosity or ill will. I don't think your position necessarily includes those. I just think you're disinclined, *ceteris paribus*, to give someone of the male persuasion the benefit of the doubt in any given situation, and that that constitutes a predisposition against men. I can't see why that's so scandalous."

"It's scandalous because you're saying I'm prejudiced when I'm not, and because you humiliated me at dinner in front of our friends."

"Look, I'm not saying you're aware of the predisposition. In fact, that's why I brought it up in the first place—because I think you're *not* aware of it. With regard to the venue, I chose that time and locale based on the immediacy of the thought. I've noticed the issue in the past, but I have an admitted tendency to forget this kind of thing should I wait too long to mention it."

Weighty footfall crosses the room. Hinges squeak on a closet door before squealing shut.

"So, I'm supposed to accept this kind of treatment because you can't get your mnemonic fitness in order? How is that fair?"

"Who said anything about 'fair'? This isn't about relativistic moral constructs. This is about you seeming to think that what I said implies that I was passing judgment on you. I wasn't trying to assign any kind of value to your predisposition. I was simply making a statement of fact based on my observations of your behavior."

"That's beside the point. I'm not upset because of what you said. If that's really what you think of me, we can have that conversation. I'm upset because you made me look like an idiot in front of our friends and because you clearly didn't think of my feelings before you said what was on your mind. You could have just as easily written yourself a note and brought it up once we got home. It's about reading the room and being a decent person, and the fact that you have difficulty with one or both of those. Did you see Kendra and Howard's faces? They were mortified."

Manly palms slap the sides of manlier thighs, having fallen from shoulder height.

"Why should I act any differently in front of our friends? If I have something to say to you, what difference does it make where we are or in front of whom it's said? I don't have any interest in compromising my integrity just to maintain some facade for the sake of other people's delicate sensibilities."

"When you do things like this, it makes me feel like you don't respect me."

"I respect you more than I respect anyone else, and you should know that. Why else would I be so frank with you? To my mind, there's no greater sign of respect than honesty, and no one can accuse me of not being honest with you."

"No one would dare."

Wood scrapes against wood as something is retrieved from a drawer.

"I choose my words very carefully, and I opt to remain silent if what I would say isn't exactly what I mean. There are always words fitting enough to quash the urge to resort to euphemism. If others are too weak to look reality in the face, it's no problem of mine."

"Don't be so hard on the rest of the world. Not everyone has your unflinching strength of character."

"Well, what would you have me do? If you're telling me I need to put on kid gloves and coddle you, I'll do it. It's just a little disappointing that you're more beholden to the pressures of societal whim than I thought you were."

"You know what? Fuck you. I'm going to take a shower. You should think about sleeping on the couch."

The bathroom door clicks as it closes, and again shortly thereafter. Bedsprings creak victory under a lonesome man.

Downstairs, the two men continue in their work, unheard.

"What a couple of assholes," Oscar rasps over to Ryan, who is turning a silver platter over and over in gloved hands. "I thought they'd never shut up."

"Assholes or not, they've got good taste. This isn't plated." Ryan whispers back, demonstrating great care as he slides the platter into a large duffel bag splayed open on the spotless kitchen floor. "Now, quit eavesdropping and grab those rings next to the sink," he says, indicating a half dozen gold bands stacked around the neck of a small porcelain giraffe near the soap dispenser. "I'm going to raid the pantry and see if they have any truffles."

"The chocolate kind or the fungal kind?" Oscar asks, eyes asparkle.

The shadow of a smile crawls into the corner of Ryan's mouth. "Cross your fingers for both."

Egg

We found a robin's nest on the sidewalk. I didn't know it was a robin's nest, but she did; she said she knew about these things. The nest had fallen out of a tree which overhung the sidewalk and threatened to strangle itself in the power lines overhead. The nest looked like it had been stepped on before we found it; all of the eggs were crushed but one. The egg rolled away when I tried to pick it up, but I snagged it before it fell through some grating. I think it might have wanted to explore the sewer.

We took the egg home with us. Not right away: we still had grocery shopping to do. I didn't want to carry the egg around in my hand in the store, because what if they thought I was trying to steal it? She said I was being silly, because they didn't sell robin's eggs there. She didn't want to put it in her purse, because it would probably break and get robin's egg yolk all over the inside. I told her I didn't think other people could identify robin's eggs as well as she could; they might just think it was one of the kinds of eggs they did sell. She told me we'd have to risk it. I agreed and carried the egg in my hand.

We walked down a few aisles and got the things we needed. We'd made a list so it would go quickly and so we wouldn't buy things we didn't need. Also, neither of us liked browsing in the supermarket. Farmers' markets were a different story entirely, but this was not one of those. We picked up some flour, sugar, and eggs (chicken), but they didn't have the kind of cheese we liked. We did not get any kind of cheese.

The checkout line was longer than we'd expected it to be. From the looks of it, a lot of people in front of us hadn't made lists. Sometimes people let you go in front of them if you only have a few items; the people in line had obviously never heard of the custom, so we waited. When we were second in line, the lady in front of us disagreed with the boy at the cash register about the price of cauliflower. It took forever for the manager to come; it turned out that the lady was wrong. She let the manager keep the cauliflower. Then it was our turn; when the cashier boy was almost done scanning our items, he asked me what I had in my hand. I said it was a robin's egg that we'd brought in from outside. He said that we'd have to pay for all of the eggs we wanted to take with us. She chimed in to assure the cashier boy that it was definitely a robin's egg (she knew about these things) and that they didn't sell them there. He said he'd have to call the manager again. We paid the chicken egg price for it so we could just leave. She was incensed that we had to pay for our own robin's egg. I thought it was a fair bargain.

She started putting the groceries away when we got home; I tried to figure out what to do with the robin's egg. I grabbed an old maroon sweater and took it into our combination office and storage room. It had really become just a storage room, but we had a hard time admitting that. I made a nest out of the sweater; the egg went into the nest, and the nest went up on top of the filing cabinet. She must have finished putting the groceries away, because she was standing next to me and looking at the nest. She said it was a good idea, but she didn't think it was going to be warm enough. I went to the garage to retrieve the infrared lamp that had briefly belonged to our pet lizard. He had looked cold in his terrarium, so I went out one afternoon and bought the lamp for him; I set it up in a hurry before we went out to dinner that same evening. I think I probably mounted it too low, because we came home to the smell of expired lizard. We mounted it higher this time.

We checked on the egg twice a day; on the third day, I thought something was happening, because the egg was in a different position. She told me that nothing was happening; she had moved the egg so it would get a little more warmth. I was disappointed. Six days later, nothing had happened and we were about ready to give up. Four days after that, the egg hatched. It turned out not to be a robin. She seemed pretty let down about that, so I didn't point out that she'd been wrong. The bird was yellow and squat with stubby wings and a beak that was lined with what looked like little teeth. I would have said the bird was deformed, but somehow it seemed like it was supposed to look like that. We named it "the bird".

The bird was hungry. We figured that out because it cheeped non-stop until we got it something to eat. We had some bird seed left over from the winter; I went out to the shed to get the bag. The bird did not like the bird seed; it refused to touch the stuff and vomited all over the top of the filing cabinet. I wasn't sure where the vomit could have come from, because the bird hadn't eaten anything yet. The following days were spent establishing things through trial and error. We tried feeding it worms, which it ate. We also tried crickets; those worked, too. In fact, the bird seemed to eat just about everything except bird seed. I noticed at one point that it had even gnawed the edges off of the filing cabinet and eaten part of its nest. It also ate steak.

The bird outgrew its nest two weeks after hatching. We moved it down to the floor of the combination office and storage room so it could run around; it seemed fine with the move at first, but then it started getting finicky about its food. We were concerned when the bird stopped eating worms. We were even more concerned when it stopped eating crickets. This pattern continued until the straw that broke the camel's back: we could not endure the bird's dereliction of steak. She went into the kitchen to call a veterinarian; I went to the living room see if there was any useful information in the encyclopedia. There was not. She came into the living room and said the vet couldn't help us; also, he had sounded a little incredulous at her description of the bird. We returned to the combination office and storage room, only to find the bird most of the way through eating an electric fondue set we'd received as a gift three Christmases prior. It didn't seem like the kind of thing a bird should eat, but the bird was clearly enjoying it. We were glad.

We observed a progressive emptying of the combination office and storage room; the bird grew accordingly. It didn't take long before the bird was bigger than I was and everything in the combination office and storage room had been eaten. We called it the birdroom after that. We didn't call it that to other people; that was just what we called it when we talked to each other about anything involving that room. We thought the new name was fitting; we were also thankful that we no longer had to live a lie.

In true two-birds-one-stone fashion, we kept the bird fed and decluttered the rest of the house of all the other useless stuff we had. One day while I was feeding it a volume of the encyclopedia, the bird bit off the end my middle finger. I was surprised at how little it hurt; I was also surprised at how easily the bird's teeth had gone through the bone. The bird swallowed the finger piece and lapped up the blood that had dripped on the floor; it didn't seem interested in the encyclopedia after that. It didn't seem interested in any of the other junk I had brought in, either. I went out on a limb and offered my index finger to the bird to see if it wanted to bite the end off of that one. It did.

She and I have been taking turns feeding the bird. I still have my entire left arm; I think it might have been a mistake to let the bird eat my legs, because now I'm having some difficulty getting around. She has her legs—no toes—and both of her arms above the elbows. She regrets letting the bird nibble her eyelids off, adorable though it was at the time; she's a much lighter sleeper now, even with a sleep mask. The bird has just about outgrown the birdroom: it can cross the room in three strides and has to stoop to keep its head from bumping against the ceiling. We spend a great deal of our time in there now; it's really become the thing we have most in common with each other, and it makes our hearts soar to see the bird thriving the way it is. We've been thinking about moving into the birdroom full-time; we figure we have only so much time left with the bird, and we want to make it count. It's a pretty tough decision to make, though, as it's not the kind of thing we'd be able to go back on.

Then again, you can't really go wrong with something done out of love.

Habitation

———

Dearest Victoria,

Arrived in Florence this morning. Rail journey was plea-surable, if somewhat overlong. Exhaustion setting in, hope telegram suffices. More to follow.

Be well, darling.

Yours always,
Quincy

———

Victoria, My Love,

Accommodations here quite breathtaking, sending charcoal sketch via post. Have been treated with utmost courtesy and care since arrival; Italians undeserving of poor reputation they endure elsewhere.

Luncheoned with Beretta this afternoon. Anticipate he will prove valuable friend in future.

Faithfully,
Quincy

━━━━━━━━━━

Dear Victoria,

Received letter from our ambassador, indicates some confusion with Italians as regards my status here. Have been moved to sub-standard lodging for interim. Block of flats fairly dilapidated, situated beneath footbridge. Fireplace in new residence of some consolation.

Rumors of falling out between ambassadors as yet unconfirmed. Pray they remain so.

Yearningly,
Quincy

━━━━━━━━━━

My Beloved Victoria,

Found whole ham in fireplace this morning. Tenement shares wall with structure of promenade above, chimneys nearly identical to municipal refuse bins. Superintendent fairly blasé about incident, insisted ham still edible. Allowed him to take it home.

Must admit to becoming a bit unnerved. Beretta unreachable of late.

Pining for you,
Quincy

Darling Victoria,

Room not square. Realization took time in coming, impossible to ignore now. Doubt I will grow accustomed. Currently avoiding acutely angled corner of domicile to minimize claustrophobia. As one spending most of life in box, would rather know box is symmetrical.

Neighbor girl came calling, no older than six. Asked for any unneeded food scraps.

Still no word from embassy or Beretta.

Counting the days,
Quincy

My Angel, Victoria,

Room filled with smoke yesterday, discovered discarded hobbyhorse blocking flue. Toy did not survive extraction. Pity, would have made lovely present for neighbor girl.

Finally received word from embassy, not good. Italians becoming erratic, distrustful. Would prefer to leave; ambassador implied departure would likely engender more enmity. Wish I had insight from Beretta.

Staying for now,
Quincy

V,

Wages not paid, message suffers. Still safe. Miss you dearly. Sorry so brief.

-Q

Victoria, My Only,

Beretta reestablished contact, previously detained by authorities. Involvement with yours truly regarded as possible security risk. Will need to abstain from English in coming months. Tension palpable.

Bottle of grappa found in fireplace three days ago, mostly full. Emptied with Beretta's help.

Longingly,
Quincy

My Precious Victoria,

Beretta concerned for my well-being should I stay much longer. Bellicose faction in parliament gaining strength. Will do my best to facilitate peace, but war may soon be upon us.

Recovered kitten from fireplace this afternoon, named it Ash. Neighbor girl tickled pink.

Hopefully,
Quincy

———————

Sweet Victoria,

Ash in fireplace this morning, nothing to be done.

War or no, had quite enough of this rubbish. Beretta arranging passage. Returning home.

Presently,
Quincy

———————

Official Post

The letter arrived despite Sarah's conviction that it never would. It had even come with a twin. They lay there on the dining table, their institutional brown paper envelopes clashing with the rainbow-crocheted tablecloth and making her wonder what the government had against white.

She lifted one of the rough little rectangles and flipped it over, but as soon as she began to peel up the flap, she knew she wasn't ready. She put it back in its place on the table. The corner of the envelope was flared where she'd inserted her finger, and it looked like a tiny mouth booing at her.

Three years earlier, Sarah hadn't realized that she would have to work so hard to become a psychologist. More precisely, she hadn't realized that she'd have to work so hard to become a psychologist *again*; she'd already been one for years back at home, but after emigrating to Taldonia, she'd been informed that she was no longer seen as qualified to practice.

The Taldonian language wasn't the issue; she'd already mastered that aspect of her adoptive culture as part of her ongoing attempt at assimilation. She also clearly had the requisite skill set, as the government had been allowing her to practice provisionally while the responsible agency went about reviewing her application for a permanent license, albeit with the requirement that she apply for a renewal of her temporary license every three to six months. She couldn't see the sense in allowing her to work before an official decision had been made, especially in light of the fact that she could theoretically renew the temporary license indefinitely, but she needed to earn a living and didn't want to jinx the situation by bringing up the inconsistency.

In the early days of the process, she'd been in frequent contact with the licensing board's central information office, which was apparently staffed entirely by people who desperately wanted to help her, but who were also adamant about their utter inability to do so.

Isn't the job the same everywhere? she had always asked. They had agreed with every word. *Isn't mental health stateless?* she had implored. They had concurred without reservation. She eventually lost count of how many times she'd been transferred to a supervisor.

After two years of non-answers, requests for notarized documents, and general evasiveness on the part of those who should have been able to fix her problem, Sarah had grown tired of jumping through hoops. In addition to being a nuisance in its own right, her lack of a fully-recognized credential was impacting her ability to secure a long-term residence visa and plan for her future security. She'd looked up a roster of employees at the licensing board, and after selecting one of the few bureaucrats with whom she hadn't yet spoken, she'd sent a firmly-worded letter requesting a final decision with regard to her status.

In the intervening time, Sarah had focused on her work and tried to make sure she could relax at home. The former was generally easier than the latter, but her backyard garden had proved to be an ideal place for her to practice unwinding, especially after she'd decided to build the deck. She'd asked her neighbor what kind of permit she would need before breaking ground, as she had seen him build an addition onto the back of his house the previous spring. He'd told her that applying for a permit would be a waste of her time and money, seeing as the city never followed up on them, anyhow. He'd then offered to build the deck for her in exchange for a few six-packs of beer, which she'd thought was very neighborly of him. When she'd asked what it would cost her to add another bathroom to the ground floor of her house, he'd upped his price by one disused moped; as luck had it, there had been one parked in her side yard for just shy of a year. Her neighbor had given her a list of things to order at the hardware store, and Christmas came early when the truck had arrived a few days later to drop the materials off on the parking pad in front of her house.

Sarah was impressed by the quality of the work her neighbor did, and while she didn't understand why he'd chosen to work on both projects simultaneously, the bathroom oasis and backyard haven were each taking shape more quickly than she could have hoped.

The job had nearly been finished when Sarah's neighbor didn't show up at the arranged time one morning. After trying to reach him directly, she'd asked around the neighborhood to see if anyone had heard from the man. The scatterbrained woman across the street had been nearly positive that he'd gotten himself locked up for smuggling fireworks and cigarettes in from the neighboring country.

After a week of staring at the missing planks of the deck and the raw drywall in her new bathroom, it occurred to

Sarah that she might be able to finish the job herself. She'd watched her neighbor work before his incarceration, and his tools were all still there, so she decided to give it a shot. A handful of helpful online videos had guided her through the rough patches that cropped up along the way, and after a few short weeks, she was able to hang up her tool belt. It had been one of the proudest moments of her life.

That feeling of accomplishment had stayed with her throughout the year, and in combination with the incomparable hours of relaxation she'd spent out on her deck, it had almost made her wish she'd left well enough alone on the licensure front. She'd gotten used to the constant renewal applications, and she'd even streamlined the process to minimize the discomfort it caused her. Then the letters had arrived.

Sarah knew that the missives weren't going anywhere, and that waiting any longer wasn't going to change whatever awaited her within. In a flash of resolve, she snatched the booing letter up again and ripped it open, letting the envelope flutter back onto the table as she read:

Dear Ms. Wenderly,

This letter serves as final notification as to the outcome of your recent application for recognition of your professional credentials.

We regret to inform you that no such recognition is possible at this time.

In order for this department to issue a full and valid certification to practice psychology within the Federal Union of Taldonia, it will be necessary for you to attend and complete a qualified credentialing program at an accredited university (please see attached list). Any such program must have a duration of no fewer than three but no more than five years.

This notification supersedes any and all previously arranged agreements, which are henceforth invalidated. If you are currently practicing under a temporary certification, you will be required to provide documented proof that all such professional activity has ceased within fifteen (15) calendar days of the date of this notification.

Please direct any questions you may have to the Central Information Office listed on the opposite side of this correspondence.

Sincerely,

Robert Leerkopf
Citizen Liaison
Office of Professional Records
Department of Unified Citizen Services

In a daze, Sarah took a seat at the table and collected the other envelope. She tore it open with her teeth, and when her vision had come back into focus, she read:

Dear Ms. Wenderly,

In accordance with the record-sharing provision of the Liberty Act, this office recently remitted your property information to the Department of Unified Citizen Services for the purposes of professional credentialing. In the process of reviewing your file, it was established that a current, valid survey of your residential property had not yet been executed. The requisite inspection was ordered by this office and carried out at no additional cost to you.

We regret to inform you that the results of the aforementioned survey indicate that your domicile, situated on city parcel number 483-11B, has been expanded or altered without the necessary construction permits and/or environmental impact survey and is in noncompliance with building code §G148, subparagraph 3. All such expansions and/or alterations are expressly forbidden and must be removed and disassembled immediately and the domicile returned to its original, permitted condition. Failure to comply with this order within twenty-one (21) calendar days will result in fines in the amount of one thousand krowns (Kr 1,000.00), levied every fourteen (14) calendar days thereafter, with interest. Overdue payments will be subject to an administrative fee in the amount of seventy-five krowns (Kr 75.00) per calendar week.

Please remit documentation of compliance and any payment due to the address listed on the reverse side of this correspondence.

We thank you for your cooperation in this matter and look forward to serving you in the future.

Sincerely,

Sasha Klauwerai
Accounts Administrator
Office of Property Compliance
Department of Public Welfare

Moving On

There was no denying it: Coco was an adventurer. She was inquisitive, resourceful and strong-willed. She was fearless and loyal to a fault, and her voice was as big as her heart. She was also known to be an excellent judge of character. Mostly, though, she was a small dog—and she was fast. Before Edna knew it, Coco was sitting at her feet once again, sweeping dried leaves from the porch with her tail and staring expectantly at the frisbee her master had thrown just a few moments earlier. Ignoring the arthritis in her knees, Edna crouched to retrieve the bright purple disc without delay; she knew that Coco didn't like to be kept waiting.

With the frisbee airborne again and a six-pound hairball careening across the lawn after it, Edna returned her attention to the man on the ladder. Joe's frequent visits to fix this or mend that were hard for Edna to afford, especially on a fixed income, but Joe always cut her a deal. It had been over a decade since her husband Frank had passed away, God rest him, and the house had fallen into a bit of disrepair since then; she had always been a homemaker, and she didn't know her butt from a hole in the ground when it came to maintenance work. She'd gotten Joe's phone number from Mabel, who'd had nothing but good things to say about the young man. When it was clear that Coco also approved, the deal was sealed. Joe was a little rough around the edges, but his heart was in the right place and he did good work; Edna wouldn't have kicked him out of bed if she'd found him there, either. He'd been on the ladder since just after lunch. Edna asked how things were coming along, addressing the question to Joe's caboose; he called down that the gutters would be unclogged in no time.

Like many residents of Greybull, Wyoming, Joe hadn't had regular work in close to two years; after those goddamn hippie protesters had gotten the mine closed down, most of the boys in town had taken work on the oil rigs in Casper or doing construction in Jackson. Neither option was open to Joe, however, whose vertigo made even cleaning gutters an act of daring. He'd considered joining a fracking outfit, seeing as it would have kept his feet on the ground, but his sister had nixed the idea after her tap water started catching fire. In the end, it was all the same to Joe, who had no intention of leaving town while Ila Mae McCready was still around. Greybull's best and only beautician held a special place in his heart, regardless of the fact that he'd never actually gotten up the nerve to go and talk to her.

Luckily for Joe, sticking around wasn't too hard; the shortage of other able-bodied men in town meant that the local handyman market had very little in the way of competition. He snapped up odd jobs wherever he found them, and he soon had a healthy list of happy clients. Joe had been called a loser before, but no one could accuse him of being lazy; on his watch, hinges lost their squeaks, and drains ran freely. Shutters bore proud coats of fresh paint, and driveway cracks were patched at a pace that crab grass simply couldn't keep. Joe made enough scratch to keep his belly full and a roof over his head, and thanks to the under-the-table nature of the business, he didn't lose anything to Uncle Sam. He was even able to do some saving.

Things were going just fine for Joe. That is, they had been going fine until he heard that Ila Mae was leaving for Missouri. Evidently, the attrition from Greybull wasn't limited to the men in town; Ila Mae's customer base had been on the dwindle for a while, and it looked like she was going to have to close up shop. Joe heard through the grapevine that his sweetheart had applied to do make-up for the local mortuary, where business was booming. However, she'd withdrawn her application when someone pointed out that she'd need to get licensed and that she'd be touching corpses all the time. Joe heard from Edna (who had heard from Bess) that Ila Mae was going to dip into her rainy-day fund and, instead of getting those eyelash implants she'd had her heart set on, was going to move in with her aunt in St. Louis and try to get a fresh start.

With nothing left for him in town, Joe felt the sudden and overwhelming need for a change of scenery. After careful deliberation, he settled on St. Louis—purely by coincidence— and went about planning his escape from Greybull. He would need to finish the last few jobs he'd already agreed to do, but then he'd be clear to pull up root and move along. The handyman money he'd saved would cover an apartment in St. Louis for a few months, but that was about it; he'd have to get creative when it came to transportation to the Gateway City. The idea of hitch-hiking struck him as overly adventurous— he was no Coco, after all—and so he'd called his old high school friend, Tom, who had long since shipped off to

Sacramento for college and a chance to make something of himself.

Tom still lived in the Californian capital, even though his original plans had gone bust; he hadn't finished his degree because he was, for lack of a better word, bored with the whole experience. Tom had always had difficulty focusing in school and had only made the initial collegiate attempt to appease his parents, who were sure that he would be the first one in the family to break out of the working class; four years later, after torturing himself with revolving-door attendance of his classes and a string of part-time telemarketing jobs, he'd broken off his foray into academia indefinitely. In the search for something more engaging, he'd somehow landed behind the meat counter at the local supermarket. He was excited about the job, and while he wasn't allowed to butcher whole cuts on his own right away, the store's apprenticeship program promised to have him certified inside of six months.

Tom worked his ass off, with gusto. With the fruits of his labor laid out in the cooler case every morning, he found that he had no problem staying focused at his new station. The six-month training period passed quickly, and the world of butchery opened up before him: bone saw and filet knife in hand, he imagined himself a surgeon one day, a samurai another, a deranged killer every other Wednesday. His enthusiasm showed in his work, and after a sharp upswing in sales and positive customer feedback, his bosses decided that a bonus was in order.

Tom was trying to decide what to do with his windfall when he got the call from Joe. Even though the two hadn't talked in years, it didn't take long to strike up the same rapport they'd had back when they were forging each other's absence slips and pranking their tenth grade history teacher, Mr.

Horowitz. Tom said he wanted to sleep on Joe's request, and he promised to call Joe back when he'd made up his mind.

When the two got off the phone, Tom looked at the note-pad upon which he'd been listing potential uses for his bonus. Material possessions made up the bulk of the list, but they had never really been of much interest to Tom; he wasn't really sure why he'd written any down in the first place. He crossed them off first. Tuition for community college was next to be stricken from the list; it was a nice idea, but Tom knew that going back to school was a dead-end for him. The last remaining item—underlined, with a question mark—was a car. Although Tom had originally listed the car as an answer to his long bicycle commute, he liked the idea of it being a twofer. Having the chance to help somebody in need had little to recommend against it, which made the decision even easier.

Joe had indicated that his few possessions would just about fit in a large suitcase; while a sedan probably would have sufficed, Tom opted for something with a little more cargo space, just to be safe. He purchased a station wagon from its original owner's son, who claimed that his mother had only ever driven it the weekly mile and a half to and from bingo night at the senior activity center. The son had paid to have it towed from the center's parking lot the week before and indicated in the ad that no reasonable offer would be refused. Tom offered what he thought was a fairly unreasonable lowball, figuring it couldn't hurt. The man accepted outright.

As Tom peered through the steam billowing from under the hood of the car some days later, he realized that the seller's eagerness to unload the vehicle probably should have been telling. With the cracked engine block pinging and moaning up at him as it cooled into ruination, he also questioned his decision to forgo an inspection before setting out on such a long haul. There was no question, however, that it had been a mistake to take a backroad route; the narrow band of asphalt—gouged through the middle of the Great Basin Desert and bookended by mountain ranges—was singularly empty and offered no shade for miles in either direction.

Tom's phone didn't have a signal, but that didn't stop him from trying. When calling for a tow didn't pan out, he worked on keeping his cool and getting ready for a long wait; he hadn't seen another car all day, and he certainly wouldn't be walking off into the desert looking for rescue—not while he still had his emergency kit, anyway. The locking plastic tub—a remnant of the time he'd squandered on Rhonda, his alarmist ex-girlfriend—had lived a life of obscurity at the back of his bedroom closet before he'd put it in the car. The kit contained a gallon jug of distilled water, several blister-packs of batteries, canned food of various kinds, an emergency fire blanket, a dynamo-powered flashlight, a walkie-talkie, a stack of survivalist literature and a first aid kit; Tom hauled the thing out of the trunk and set it next to him on the passenger seat up front.

After stowing the water in the shadiest place he could find on the floor under the dash, Tom went about examining the rest of his supplies. The batteries were still good, but he couldn't get anything apart from static on the walkie; he'd never tested it, so he wasn't sure if it was broken or if he were running into the same issue he'd had with the phone. He decided not to open any of the food just yet, even though his stomach was beginning to growl; he'd cheaped out and bought a bunch of dented cans to fill the kit, and half of them were bulging and distended to the point that they were nearly spherical. He moved on to the fire blanket, which he used to block some of the sun's intensity from the car by tucking it behind the windshield's flip-down visors and weighing down the bottom corners with a few of the bulgy botulin incubators. After ensuring that his first aid kit was complete, he settled in with a pamphlet entitled "How to Stay Alive".

Tom was sucking on a slice of mandarin orange and fighting off nightfall with the wan illumination of his crank flashlight when he caught a glimpse of headlights in his driver-side mirror. By the time he had scrambled out of the car, he could see that there were, in fact, two sets of headlights in the distance, one behind the other. It wasn't until almost a minute later that he could distinguish the red and blue flashers hovering along above the second set of headlights.

Tom thought the reflection from his car's taillights would probably catch the incoming drivers' attention, but he wasn't willing to leave it to chance. His meager food supply might have lasted him another few days if he rationed it properly, but he had already drunk half of his water to stave off the heatstroke threatened by the desert sun. He strode to the middle of the road and, after reassuring himself that his plan wasn't insane, cranked madly at his flashlight as he pointed it in the direction of the oncoming vehicles.

As he dove out of the way of the car chase, Tom was certain that he'd been seen by the driver of the lead car. He hoped dearly that the highway patrolman following close behind had seen him, too, and that the officer would call in the cavalry on his behalf.

Officer Combes had indeed seen the man by the side of the road, and he planned on calling in the breakdown as soon as he was able. They were in the middle of a radio dead zone, though, and the call was going to have to wait until they were on the other side of the upcoming mountain pass. It would also have to wait until after he had called the babysitter; Combes was already stressed at being unable to let her know that he was going to be late. He dreaded the fortune he was going to owe her in overtime, too. He normally didn't mind giving the girl a little something extra for her trouble—she was a sweet kid, in a geeky kind of way, and he knew she was saving for a trip with her dance troupe— but things had been tight since the austerity measures in the state budget had forced him to take a pay cut. He was thankful that he hadn't been furloughed like some of the rookies had, but thankfulness wasn't going pay the bills or keep his ex-wife off his back; she was already on his case for having missed their daughter's first recital on account of the interstate drug bust he'd stumbled into the month before.

Unfortunately, letting the speed demon go wasn't an option. There had been a state-wide APB out on her for months, and she had just broken a half dozen laws right in front of him. He would never have admitted it, but there was no small measure of his pride wrapped up in the issue, as well: he had been at the top of his class in Advanced Pursuit training, but he had yet to gain any ground on the suspect. Granted, she had hit her apexes perfectly on every curve, and he imagined her pedal work was top-notch, but enough was enough. She had clearly been lucky to encounter nothing but run-of-the-mill highway troopers up until that point; it was about time for her luck to run out, and he was ready to help it along.

Pedals gave way, subservient under the fugitive's feet; the shudder and buzz of the engine climbed up through the knob in her right hand and sprinted all the way up into her brain. Euphoria. Needles swung to the right in slick arcs, and lights blinked frantically while the world streaked by, faster and faster and faster. She loved being pressed backward into leather, reveling in the strain in her neck as she fought the acceleration trying to rip her head off.

Red and blue lights flashed in the mirrors all around her, filling the cabin with an adrenaline glow. She'd never been caught, and this one wouldn't catch her, either. If these podunk towns had helicopters or drones like metropolitan law enforcement sometimes did, they might have had a chance, but hillbillies in obsolete Crown Vics were simply outgunned. Sometimes she would let them get close, give them a bit of a thrill by wiggling her tail right in their faces. Then she'd power on through the turn, kick the back end out in a snarling, squealing cacophony of tire smoke and crackling exhaust, and slingshot herself beyond their reach. It never got old, watching them try to follow as they hung on for dear life, their sorry black-and-whites coughing and sputtering as they fishtailed all over the asphalt. It served them right for thinking that they were somehow better than her simply by merit of having an extra bit of flesh dangling between their legs and a tendency to suck all the feeling out of the world. Really, they needed someone to shame them; luckily, she could think of no better use for her time than handing out life lessons to a bunch of overinflated knuckle-draggers.

One time, some doltish donut-dunker had really gone overboard in trying to imitate her art; she'd looked back just in time to see the unlucky bastard lose traction and drift his patrol car right off the edge of a canyon road. She'd never found out what happened to that one, but she hoped he hadn't died—it was one thing to disdain the cops, but quite another to wish them harm. Besides, it was much more entertaining to imagine her pursuers surviving the ordeal and having to explain to their superiors why and how it was that they had been so thoroughly flummoxed by some red-headed bimbo in a muscle car she had no business driving.

As she exited the second turn of the mountain pass and loosened her grip on the steering wheel, her mind wandered to the man with the flashlight she'd nearly run over. With sheer stone faces rising higher on either side of the road and the dust cloud she'd dragged out of the corner struggling to keep up, she wondered if the deputy she'd just evaded would double back to help the guy. Her self-congratulation over yet another successful lesson was cut short when she realized that her car's interior was still lit up like a Christmas tree; the lawman staring defiantly back at her from the rear-view mirror was sawing away at the wheel of his aging cruiser and coaxing some pretty convincing ballet from the same.

She tried to make sense of what should have been an impossible situation and, in doing so, found herself entertaining thoughts that hadn't graced her mind in years. Her heart raced and her palms broke into a sweat as she shifted down; her engine roared a crescendo, gulping fuel and spraying flames as it rocketed her onward amidst encroaching mountains and a sudden need to know what awaited her on the other side.

On the Head of a Pin

I saw the train too late I should have looked both ways I mean the lights weren't flashing but that's no excuse I really should have known better they tried to save me but it didn't work and I died there were no singing choirs triumphal no shining gates no knowing man in long white robes with long white beard and gleaming book in hand there was only the darkness first and then a deeper place and then a thin dizzy seeing one would not describe as light I did not go toward it not willingly at least because I did not want to see again but then I had to and I was here and no longer alone there were others they had not expected to be here just as I had not why would we have we never believed in any of this we never thought we would wind up seraphim but here we are and now I've got six wings somehow they got that part right but I don't have a flaming sword that would be silly they would see me coming instead I have a knife which is darker than death and it's my job to get rid of the ones who wind up here by mistake it's hard work but I do it well and besides there isn't much else to do up here except talk about the time before when we gawked at the ones who went to church and clasped their hands and bowed their heads and said the words and tried so hard to feel their hearts fill up and some did but many didn't and all got back to their feet with carpet burns on their knees and emptied their wallets so that someone they didn't know could eat a hot meal at least that's what the people holding the plate had told them but no one checks to see if it's true and anyway god doesn't want the believers they think they can get to heaven by being good and following rules but it's a catch twenty-two because no one who believes in heaven can get in it's kind of sad to watch the ones who die just wander and wander and wonder what they did wrong and why they are still there in the brown and gray world they just knew would not be the last but it turns out god does work in mysterious ways and it was foolish for us to try to say anything about his motivations or character or rules we were all wrong he is not a mean kid with a magnifying glass and an ant hill and he is not pure love he doesn't care so much if we acknowledge him or believe at all I mean he appreciates it and everything but he actually wants us not to believe so that we can focus on the earthly world because that's the test you can call it hands-off parenting or insistence upon free will or whatever you want the upshot is that purgatory is full of pious people and assholes while all the well-meaning atheists are up here wondering what the hell happened to us and what we should do now that everything we were so sure of turns out to have been so wrong we'll have to figure it out all over again I guess it's not so bad if you think about it even though I wonder if this is really the end if you know what I mean so I guess my advice to you if you want to get in is that you have to live life on your own and reason it out for yourself and be good to everyone not just the ones who are like you that's what he wants not a bunch of his children just doing what they are told for ever and ever and ever he wants to see us grow up and take responsibility for ourselves and one another and the world we live in and just get our shit together so that he can get back to doing his own thing instead of worrying about us the whole goddamn time

Dissonance

"F sharp, man. F *sharp*." Randy's voice pops and squeaks in all the wrong places, just about spent; it's not fitting for such a big guy. That was the eighth take, and the guys are making it through less and less of the song with each attempt.

"Sorry, bud, that's my bad. I got it this time." Mikey wobbles a bit as he speaks but doesn't slur the words. It's an impressive feat, considering the volume of bourbon he's put away tonight. He repositions his guitar strap and pulls out a new pick, which he promptly drops. He stares at the shiny red triangle on the floor, then pulls out another to replace the one he's dropped, seeming to have thought better of bending down to retrieve it. He rolls his head, shakes his hands out, and assumes his signature stance. "Ready to wail, gentlemen."

"No, Mikey. That's it." Nolan, the exhausted drummer, collects his sticks in one hand and leans forward onto a sweat-flecked tom.

"That's what?" Mikey snaps, whirling around to answer Nolan's fatigued gaze with fire. Mikey's left hand wrings the guitar's neck; the white-knuckled grip sends a moan of distortion crackling through his second-hand amp.

Randy steps between the two men, his back to Nolan. "Look, man, this has been going on long enough. You need to get your shit sorted out."

Mikey doesn't respond; he's still glaring at Nolan as though Randy's considerable bulk were not blocking his view.

"The last gig was a fucking disaster," Randy continues, trying to draw Mikey's eyes off of the drummer. "Do you even remember it, Mike? You started playing 'Donkified' before we even got through the bridge on 'Gigolo Crush', and then you passed out and fell into the pit. We can't afford to lose fans at this point in the game—we're not going to get those people back."

"So we lost a few dozen pussies who can't deal with a little extra rock," says Mikey, his grip on the guitar tighter than ever; he's still looking through Randy. "Do we even want them?"

"We do, Mikey. We want everyone," Randy sighs. He inhales through his nose and holds it until the looming thing tumbles out of him: "We've been talking, and we think it's time you took a break. We're worried about you, man. It'd be better for everyone if you sat out for a while."

"Bullshit, *better for everyone*," Mikey spits. "Better for who? The fuck am I gonna do, go back to busing tables? And what are you pricks gonna to do without someone on rhythm?" Mikey asks, shifting his shoulders under the weight of his instrument.

"Diego's cousin is ready to step in while you're gone," Randy says as he gestures to Diego, the perpetually silent bassist. "He doesn't have much experience on stage, but he's got some chops."

"What, that kid that came to the Buffalo show?" Mikey asks, laughing. He finally looks Randy in the face. "You gotta be fucking kidding me."

"Dead serious," Randy replies, having found his courage somewhere along the way. "This is happening, Mike."

"Fuck it," Mikey coughs as he throws up his hands. "If you guys want to sound like shit and pander to a bunch of little bitches, it's no skin off my dick."

"That's not what this is about, Mike. We just want what's best for you and the band."

Mikey remains silent. After a short pause, Randy broaches the other subject on the docket.

"There's one more thing. My girlfriend read me the riot act over the weekend, so we're moving our sessions over to Nolan's. It's not as convenient, but he's got workable space and thick walls."

"Yeah, so?" Mikey asks, unhooking the strap from his guitar.

"So, you have the van. None of us has a car big enough to move the gear."

"You're serious," Mikey says after scrutinizing Randy's face for a few seconds. "Jesus, you got some fucking balls on you."

"Look, I thought it would be in bad taste to have you help us move the stuff first. If you don't want to do it…"

"No, I'd love to do it!" Mikey exclaims with a bow. "Why wouldn't I want to schlep your shit around for you after you just kicked me out of the band?"

"Like I said, this is supposed to be temporary. It's up to you how long it's going to last," Randy shrugs. "So, can you help us out?"

"I'll move the stuff," Mikey says, throwing his keys into Randy's chest and turning to head for the door. "You're loading up, though. I'm going for a walk."

"If it makes a difference, I'm sorry things played out like this," Randy calls after him.

"It doesn't," Mikey mutters back. He doesn't break stride.

When he returns half an hour later, he finds the guys loading the last of the cables into the van. He hangs back and smokes a cigarette until they're finished, then approaches Randy to retrieve his keys.

"Cool if I ride shotgun?" Randy asks, dropping the keyring into Mikey's palm.

"I'm gonna drive this one alone," Mikey replies, shaking the keys into order as he heads for the driver's side.

Randy starts to say something that winds up coming out as "Nuh". He casts a helpless look over to Diego, who says nothing.

"What, you don't trust me?" Mikey demands. "You ask me to do you a favor and then you're gonna fucking insult me to my face? How 'bout this? Fuck this whole thing. Get your shit outta my vehicle."

"No, Mike, it's not that. It's cool," Randy says hurriedly. "I just wanted to make sure you're good to drive."

"What, the booze? I'm not a fucking lightweight," says Mikey, his anger subsiding slightly. "And I haven't even hit it that hard tonight."

"It's fine, forget it," says Randy in a mollifying tone. "You remember how to get there from here, yeah?"

"Yeah," Mikey nods. "East on seventy-eight for a while. Across from that one strip joint we used to go to."

"You got it. We'll meet you there."

"I gotta fill up first," Mikey warns as he climbs into the driver's seat. "Don't freak out if it takes me a bit."

Mikey decides to take surface streets over to Nolan's; the highway hasn't been repaved in years, and he doesn't want to wreck his shocks or the gear sitting in back. Besides, there's a cheap gas station only a few blocks away that carries the brand of jerky he likes.

He pulls into the station and checks that the cargo doors are locked. The central locking on the van hasn't worked since he bypassed a fuse for the cooling fan, so he has to use the key every time. Sometimes he forgets. This would be a bad time to forget.

He lets the pump do its thing while he heads into the Quik-Mart; he unloads something gnarly in the bathroom and grabs two bags of teriyaki jerky on his way back out to the van. The receipt for the gas goes into his shirt pocket—it'll go to the guys once he gets where he's going.

Mikey's mind wanders as he drives the rest of the way to Nolan's, and he tries to figure out what the hell he's going to do with all the extra time he's about to have. At one point, he veers out of his lane and nearly hits a cyclist, who swerves clear of the van and skids to a stop on the soft shoulder. Mikey flips him the bird and yells that roads are for cars.

He crests the final hill of the trip and rides the brakes on the way down. He can see Nolan's place on the left, a turn-of-the-century Dutch colonial with mismatched shingles and neighbors who are prone to domestic incidents. The lights are on at Nolan's, but none of the guys are waiting outside. Mikey thinks it could be a gesture of trust, but he also doesn't feel like parking and going in to get them. He decides he's not in the mood to be patronized and lets his foot off the brake.

Half an hour later, he's on the other side of town trying to find a parking spot in front of the Brookline. It's one of his regular haunts; they pour heavy and don't make small talk if you don't want it.

Nicole is on duty behind the ancient mahogany slab that runs the length of the narrow room. She and Mikey have never slept together, despite Mikey's regular advances. He sometimes wonders if she's a dyke, but it doesn't stop him from trying.

Mikey is on his third rye when George, one of the regulars, sidles over and hops up onto the seat to Mikey's right. George is known to ramble, which is the kind of thing that usually gets on Mikey's nerves, but tonight Mikey's just fine with letting someone else's thoughts fill his mind for a while.

"That's what I like about vinyl," George says after a needlessly long preamble. "It reminds me of back when you really interacted with your music, when it wasn't disposable. It was heavy, and it took up space in your living room. You read liner notes. Now, you throw three thousand songs on a little chip, and you play everything all mixed up, and there's no soul to it. Hell, back then you had to exercise to listen to music. It was a chore, but it was so good that it was worth getting up off your ass to flip the record so you could keep listening."

"Preachin' to the choir," Mikey echoes into his glass.

"You used to have a relationship with your music, you know what I mean? You had this shared history—it left its mark on you, and you left your mark on it. I got this one scratch in my copy of Machine Head—I brought it to a buddy's house party, and Trina got plastered and insisted on flipping to the B-side. I was fucking pissed at her at the time—I hardly knew her and she just wrecked my favorite album—but now every time I hear that pop, it takes me right back to that night. She gave me head after everyone else left. Best blowjob I ever had."

Mikey notices the wedding ring George is wearing; an index finger unfolds from the crook of Mikey's elbow to convey the realization.

"Oh, yeah, me and Trina got hitched a while back," George says, flaring the fingers of his left hand; he leans into confiding range. "I love the girl, and she works hard, but she still hasn't topped that hummer."

Nicole comes over around six drinks in and asks the boys to close their tabs; she's off at the end of the hour and has somewhere to be.

"Who's taking over?" Mikey asks, hoping for Celine.

"Pete," says Nicole. Mikey decides it would be best to move along: he and Pete don't see eye to eye on account of Mikey having never called Pete's sister after that one time. He tips Nicole well and asks if she needs a ride home. She shuts him down.

As Mikey hauls himself up into the van, he pulls his phone out to check the time. It's late, and he has twelve missed calls and almost as many text messages. He clears the calls and does a batch delete on the messages. He already knows what they say, and it makes him smile to know those fuckers are squirming.

There's no doubt that he's way over the limit, but there's even less doubt that he's not ready to call it a night. He'll just have to nut up and focus for the five or so minutes it takes to get over to the Celtic Coast. They're not as generous with the drinks over there, and no one knows him by name, but he doesn't have beef with any of the guys tending bar. He lets out an eye-watering belch, slaps himself a few times in the face, and reaches down to turn the ignition.

A few close calls and a poor parking job later, Mikey crosses the threshold of the Coast; he plops down and orders a double from the guy behind the bar, who he thinks is named Henry. There are a handful of other patrons in the place, silent little islands in a sea of stale beer. At one point, a woman gets up and stumbles to the exit; she leans against the inside of the open door, swinging her head sluggishly from left to right in a way that someone who knows which way to go would not. Her knees stop wobbling long enough for her to take a step, and she's off. Mikey's eyes track her outline across the frosted glass of the front window.

"She's a sad song, isn't she?" Mikey asks no one in particular; he looks back to the window just in time to see the woman's silhouette heading jerkily in the other direction.

Three drinks later, Mikey is the only one left in the bar besides the bartender, who is drying a pint glass with a greasy towel. Mikey asks if the game is on.

"Already over," maybe-Henry says, glancing up at the TV. "Eagles lost by six."

"I meant the other game," Mikey says as he inclines his head toward the back of the bar.

The bartender continues smearing the glass with the towel as he squints at Mikey; apparently satisfied that he isn't a cop, the man points his elbow in the direction Mikey indicated. "Go on back."

Mikey tucks a twenty under his glass, slides off his stool, and saunters to the rear of the bar. He heads left down a dim corridor and comes to a heavy steel door with a rainbow of profanity scribbled on it; he knocks and is immediately greeted by an oversized man with a deep scar over his right eye and a brick for a chin.

"Here to play," Mikey says, trying hard not to slur as he retrieves his wallet from his back pocket.

"Five hundred minimum buy-in tonight," growls the Golem.

"Five hundred? It's usually fifty," Mikey says, searching his billfold for cash he knows isn't there.

"Then come back when it's fifty," the man grunts as he moves to close the door again.

"Hold up," Mikey interjects, his hand splayed against a crudely drawn scrotum. "I'll just open a tab."

"No house credit for walk-ins," the man says. "Probably got time to go rob a wall if you want."

"Rather not," Mikey dodges, recalling the overdraft notice wedged between his sofa cushions. "You take collateral?"

"Depends what you got. Whatever it is, you gotta have it in hand. Like I said, we don't do IOUs."

Mikey contemplates the mountain of gear sitting in the van out front. Then he weighs the likelihood that the guys are actually intending on letting him back into the band. The way forward is clear.

"Tell 'em to deal me in."

Songs for Yuoai

It is hard to know just how it starts, but know this: it starts of its own accord, and with a groan. Day dawns, a cock crows, clouds part and a burning infant sun claws its way up to sit on a listing horizon. Waking in a room of no particular form and of no particular import, you cry without control until calm falls to drown your sobs in a nothing you call your own. You think about a Monday, four days prior, on which you did not stop your hand from bringing that glass to your lips, did not stop your brain from inviting that wondrous poison in for a visit. "Just a quick visit," your mind had said, "for this body must work tomorrow." Work is but a distant thought today, for your poison pays your mind no mind; it talks without stopping and knows no words but "now".

A book, worn with worry, waits on your night-stand-cum-daystand, sitting in a shaft of vagrant light which hurts to look upon. *Songs for Yuoai* looks back up at you and sighs as you lift it from its coat of thick gray dust. Gulping and blurry did you last scan its songs that long ago and hazy night, looking for a bright tooth in this mouth of mortal sorrow. Words did spring and sway and float from your lap, binding and ink all digging into your thighs. But spring and sway and float as words might, on that night no words could pull you in, no words could bring your soul to stir. Down in that book, lush grass did grow. Down in that book, crisp snow did fall. Down in that book, warm passion did bloom and crystal rain did flow down mountain crags. Up in your failing world, two stark, dark words did form in your throat to gag you with a lucid truth:

"I can't."

Gutting and triumphant and frantic as it is, humanity's part in this play is but a walk-on. Our stay on this rock is imaginary, our mourning and our joy hallucinations of worth in a world without any. You may do what you will with that stay, but should you stop to ask, wisdom will thus insist:

Do not stay too long.

Lucky Bastard

Petrioli kept the place dark on purpose. Sure, there were caged display windows on the storefront—you'd have to be crazy to run a pawn shop and not show off some of the wonderful, sad things that people part with—but the windows were sealed on the backside, and the shop's interior was lit only by a dim, overhead fluorescent tube. It may have been dismal, but Petrioli felt he could negotiate better in the setting; he'd never had anyone walk out of his shop carrying what they had brought in.

He sat behind the counter, hunched over and polishing a diamond engagement ring a young man had pawned earlier that morning. It seemed the lady in his life had thought better of it, and the jewelry store where the poor guy had bought the thing had a less than generous return policy. Petrioli had offered the kid forty bucks for it, which was a little less than what the thin gold band was worth at wholesale. Diamonds themselves were effectively worthless on account of huge oversupply, as everyone in the business knew. The diamond cartels did a good job of convincing the public that the little stones were rare, though, and people still seemed willing to cough up crazy money for the things at retail. The sap with the ring wound up taking forty-five, the extra five being necessary to get him to swallow his indignation about the diamond. It turned out to be of surprisingly good quality for a commercial stone, and Petrioli now found himself enjoying the little fleck of carbon under his loupe. Worthless or not, the thing was pretty. Just as he was about to lean in for a closer look at one of the facets, squeaking hinges from across the room broke the silence in the shop, and the gem exploded in brilliant light. The front door stood open, pouring a column of midday sun into the space.

The stocky figure silhouetted in the doorway wasted no time, shutting the door behind him and walking so briskly toward Petrioli that the pawnbroker shrank and nearly dropped the ring he was holding. The man stopped abruptly in front of the counter, extended his right hand and flashed a grin.

"Hello, my name is Bastian, and I was wondering if you could help me with something." The stranger wore a stark white tailored suit with a black shirt and onyx cufflinks. His mane of immaculate auburn hair, snakeskin shoes, and freshly manicured nails suggested he was a man of leisure.

Petrioli, who had quickly composed himself and packed the ring away, took the man's hand and gave it a quick, confident pump. "Jim Petrioli," he said in the deepest and surest voice he could muster. A show of weakness was not a good way to start negotiations.

"Pleased to meet you, Mr. Petrioli," the stranger said, his grin unwavering.

"Well, let's see if we can find what you need, Mr.... Sebastian, right?"

"No, it's *Bastian*," the man said, lingering on the hiss in the middle of the word. "There's no 'S-E' at the front. Just Bastian."

"Bastian. Huh," Petrioli said, his lower lip jutting slightly. "Never heard that before."

"No worries, it's a German name."

"Oh, yeah? Your parents German?"

"Indeed, they are," the stranger said. "To be fair, so am I. I'm from Berlin, just here on holiday. It's a working holiday, I suppose."

"No shit? You don't sound German. I coulda sworn you was British or somethin'."

"Cheers!" the man said brightly. "That's always nice to hear. I lived in England for a year or so. The West Midlands, Coventry. Do you know the area?"

"Never been overseas," Petrioli replied, almost defensively. "Always wanted to go to Spain. Met a Spanish girl when I was younger—kinda girl that makes you want to break the law, you know? Real adventurous." The echo of rebellion in Petrioli's voice was unmistakable. "After she left town, I thought I should see what kinda place someone that pretty and mean comes from. There coulda been more like her, right? But, life happened. Never made it over there."

"That's a shame," the stranger said sympathetically. "I can't recommend Spain enough."

"Anyway, enough of this yappin'," Petrioli said with a wave of his hand. "What can I do for you, Bastian?"

"Well, Mr. Petrioli, it's fairly simple," the man replied. "You can die."

The man called Bastian turned on his heel and deftly removed his coat, hanging it on a screw protruding from one of the freestanding shelves in the shop. In doing so, he exposed the burled walnut grip and glinting steel barrel of an almost comically long revolver, which was tucked under his right armpit and ran almost the entire length of his torso, stopping just a few scant inches above his snakeskin belt. The man took a moment to brush the wrinkles out of the jacket with the backs of his hands and then turned back around. When he did so, he found himself staring down the barrel of Petrioli's comparatively short, but still sufficiently deadly, Colt 1911.

The stranger, unfazed, made no move for the cannon at his side. "I wouldn't do that, Mr. Petrioli. It wouldn't work out in your favor."

"I already shot two punks tryin' to rob me this year. You think I won't put you in the ground, you got somethin' else comin'." Petrioli's eyes, angry and sorry, did not lie.

"Oh, I'm not here to rob you, Mr. Petrioli," the man chuckled, straightening. "I'm here to restore balance."

"Wait a minute—did Wyler send you? I told that bastard I'd get him the money by next week. I still got four days to get the rest." Petrioli's hand was beginning to shake slightly; the stranger's eyes followed the business end of the Colt in little loops.

"You seem to have the wrong idea," the stranger said plaintively. "I'm not some hired thug, and I certainly don't want anything material from you. I'm simply an agent of order in the world."

"I got no idea what the hell you're talkin' about. Now, why don't you pick up your shit and walk back out that door, nice and slow?" Petrioli nodded at the man's coat and flicked the end of his gun toward the front of the shop.

"I'm going to have to stay, I'm afraid. Perhaps I should explain," the stranger offered. He raised his hands, palms facing each other and fingers splayed, as if he were carrying this explanation in a box. "You see, there are these little pockets in the universe where things don't work quite as they should. The laws of physics and probability start to break down, and any semblance of order goes with them. I go around and close these pockets so they don't spread too much and make the world an unpleasant place to be. I try to be quick about my work, as small pockets are much easier to close than large ones. One of these pockets, a very small one, is inside of you, I'm afraid, and I need to get in there to collapse it before it grows. Unfortunately, you won't survive the experience. If you'll allow me, I can end your life quickly and do the procedure afterward. So you don't have to suffer, I mean. Believe me, this is the best offer you're going to get. The chaos growing inside you won't afford you such a gentle end."

"Listen, freak," Petrioli said, adjusting his grip on the gun, "you got to the count of three to get the fuck out of my shop, or I'm gonna ventilate you."

"Please, Mr. Petrioli," the stranger replied, an index finger raised in polite protest. "Jim. Let's not."

"One."

"This is a mistake," the man said pleadingly. "You don't want to do it this way. This way hurts."

"Two."

"All right. It looks like you're not going to be persuaded. Please keep in mind that I tried." The stranger slowly extended his arms toward Petrioli, his middle and index fingers forming mirrored "L" shapes as his eyes narrowed and his jaw clenched. He looked like a cinematographer, concentrated on framing a shot.

"THREE."

The stranger's eyes snapped wide open, and a sudden, powerful vibration pervaded the shop.

Petrioli pulled the trigger. He felt the familiar kick of the Colt in his hand, and he saw the slide move out of the way of the expelled casing. Something was different, though—everything felt somehow slower, like time had been stretched out, a rubber band between fingertips. He could see the stranger, head cocked and consternated look on his face, pull the giant revolver from his side and draw up on him. The man called Bastian seemed entirely unaffected by the vibration; his movements were fluid and unhindered, accompanied by flashed hints at which direction he might move should he choose to do so in the infinity available to him. He seemed to contemplate Petrioli's bullet, still only a few inches out of the Colt's barrel, exhaust gases pushing a violent mushroom out behind it.

The stranger pursed his lips and let out a high, thin whistle; hard black lines slid out of the two men's guns, the initial paths of their respective bullets. At the point where these lines met in the middle, a loom of possible trajectories spilled out across the room, each potential path manifest in a bright white strand which hung in the air and ran around the interior of the shop, touching various objects and either terminating or continuing off in some other direction. With each slight movement that the stranger made, new webs would burst forth. Lines faded or disappeared completely as the pawnbroker's bullet made slow forward progress, but the man called Bastian didn't show any signs of rushing the act. He tilted his gun hand this way and that, did a little squat, studied the way the bullets would race around him and where they would eventually find a home. After much lip-biting, eye-squinting and head-shaking, he was standing roughly two large steps back and a small step to the right of where he had originally stood. Apparently satisfied with his choice, the stranger steadied the gun in his left hand and took a deep breath. He raised his empty right hand to shoulder height and, with his middle finger and thumb, snapped his fingers at the same moment he pulled the revolver's trigger.

Time jerked back to normal speed, and the room burst into cacophonous dance. The crack of the gunshots rang around the concrete room; a tuba shook, a large pipe wrench swayed, a bowling ball spun in place on its shelf. The commotion was punctuated by a sharp and sudden heat just above the shop-keeper's navel. With fumbling fingers, Petrioli pulled up the hem of his faded blue cardigan. There were two small holes, one slightly larger than the other, next to one another and just below the ragged, U-shaped scar he'd gotten climbing a wrought iron fence when he was nineteen. The arrangement looked like a slightly stupid and very unhappy face.

The cockeyed little homunculus frowning back up at Petrioli wept increasing red down his exposed stomach; it cried the strength right out of him, and he felt his legs go all liquid and worthless as the dim light in the room rose to blinding. The next he knew, he was sitting on the floor behind the counter, a pool of steadily growing scarlet soaking his clothes and making him wish he'd taken the day off. A disembodied voice, admonishing and regretful, called out from the other side of the counter: "I told you this wouldn't turn out in your favor, Mr. Petrioli. I have a way of making things happen the way I need them to, as I'm sure you're now aware."

Petrioli heard the harsh clack of unhurried boot heels on the shop's linoleum floor. The man called Bastian lifted the hinged portion of the counter and strode around to where Petrioli was slumped against the wall. He slid the pawnbro-ker's pistol away with the edge of his foot and raised his own weapon to the wounded man's head. The stranger looked to be on the verge of tears.

"I'm sorry about this, Mr. Petrioli," he said in a wavering voice. "Really, I am. It's just something that has to be done."

For Petrioli, there was no life flashing before his eyes, no light at the end of a tunnel. There was only the pain in his gut, pinning his arms at his sides and making his toes tingle. He looked into the void at the end of the stranger's gun and thought about what the man had said about order and chaos. He believed all of it in that moment—because he had to—and it was comforting to think that the world would be a better place because of old Jim. He couldn't have said that before, he realized, and he was thankful that this weirdo had come into his life and put some fire and a few bits of lead in his belly. Thoughts of the afterlife and whether it really existed crept into his mind from the periphery, but he shooed them away; he'd find out for sure soon enough. He heard the man called Bastian pull back the revolver's massive hammer. Then, with an uncanny *click*, Jim Petrioli was gone.

Underground

Shelly's right foot slides a little coming off the bottom stair, and she reflexively grabs for the handrail. Balancing the cardboard box on one hand, she catches the U-bend at the end of the rail with the other; it smarts, and she chips a nail, but the greater catastrophe has been averted. The last thing she needs right now is to spill the remnants of her career all over the fucking subway platform.

A busker has set up shop on the benches toward the middle of the platform. "Busker" seems like a poor fit, really—the woman is clearly a classically trained violinist and has no doubt been reduced to playing here because of some scandalous past proceeding. The woman's instrument moans a song Shelly knows, not by name, which always forces blood into a spot at the base of her throat and makes her scalp tingle. She looks around to see if the music is having a similar effect on anyone else. It is not.

There are only two other people on the platform. One very homeless gentleman has bedded down and is diligently dressing his gangrenous ankle with a scarf of questionable sterility. Another man in a tailored blue suit is staring vacuously at a station map while shitty techno music blares through his oversized headphones. Shelly decides that the homeless guy gets a pass, but feels a driving urge to run up to the suit, yank his headphones off and slap some sense into him. The violinist's song continues, unheard by two-thirds of its audience. Shelly tries to get a grip on her inclinations.

The train is delayed, which gives her unwelcome time to mull over the events of the past week. Karen, her sister, called on Tuesday to let her know that she was just diagnosed with ovarian cancer. Shelly was understandably distracted on Wednesday, but the parking cop didn't find this to be a satisfactory excuse for her failure to see the *No Parking* sign, which was quite clearly posted. Thursday was a wash. The company blindsided her at the end of work today. She'd been expecting a promotion.

When the train arrives, Shelly hangs back. The suit, on the other hand, pushes into the car without bothering to wait for the egress; it turns into a breakbeat dance that neither he nor the other passengers seem to enjoy. Eventually, lights flash and the public address warns that the doors are about to close. A few moments later, the last car of the train disappears into the tunnel. Shelly is still on the platform.

The freshly disembarked commuters ascend the stairs, and the station is as good as empty. The homeless man has disappeared into a pile of dingy blankets, and the violinist is so enthralled with the song she's playing that Shelly can't imagine the woman would notice it if a gunfight were to break out. Even the station engineer seems to have evaporated; from Shelly's vantage point, the one-way glass of the control booth is backlit, and she can see straight through.

She walks to the edge of the platform and peers down into the trench that houses the rails. Two mice are scampering along one of the ties and having an altercation over a chunk of stale bagel. One of the mice abandons the food and mounts the other, who is too thrilled with the morsel to protest. Shelly has seen the move before. She looks down the length of the track in both directions and thinks about the loss-of-control issues that some people have in high places. She lowers her cardboard box into the trench, takes a seat on the edge, and hops down onto the tracks.

The fluorescent yawn of the tunnel entrance disappears around a corner as she marches, and the crushed stone ballast between the ties shifts beneath her feet, clacking and crunching with each echoed step. After losing her balance for the third time, she sticks to the narrow strip of concrete along the left-hand side of the tracks. Her eyes adjust in time, and as the caged lamps that run along the walls grow dimmer, loomed cables and concrete pillars emerge from the dark spaces in-between.

She looks down at the box in her arms and she wishes she had given it to the homeless man back at the station. She thinks a little harder and decides that office supplies and a bunch of her workplace mementos would likely be worthless to him. The box gets heavier. She flexes her hand under its weight and wonders if she might have fractured her ring finger on the stair railing; the thought is interrupted by the sound of fabric tearing. Her left sleeve is a step behind, dawdling on an angular steel wall bracket. The blouse is brand new. Was brand new. The bracket doesn't have any apparent purpose.

The rails whine and hum for a few seconds before the vibrations arrive with a clatter, and the sight of headlights spilling around the bend does not instill fear in Shelly the way she thought it might. She moves to stand squarely between the rails, her slackened arms resting the box against her thighs. She closes her eyes and tilts her head back as the pressure wave in front of the locomotive brushes the hair gently from her shoulders. She is ready.

The service door is cold against her back, even through her blouse. Her newly exposed arm gets the worst of it. The head of a mostly functional desk lamp hovers below her chin; with her box of indispensables hugged to her chest, the recessed doorway is just deep enough for her to fit. Morse code beats in her throat, and she finds herself unable to inhale as the train speeds by, the negative air pressure threatening to suck her back out into her mistake. An endless chain of cars thunders through; windows flash into the alcove as they pass, projecting images of the things that make her life what it is. She sees her nieces in their youth, frizzy hair and unicorn pajamas, begging to watch one more movie before bed at her place in the hills. She sees her friends smiling their goodbyes after a late night of cheap wine and deep conversation. She sees Karen reaching out a tiny hand to her as they bump along through the desert on the sweaty rear seat of their parents' Bel Air on the yearly trip to Las Vegas. She sees many things. Her troubles are not among them.

At the start of his next shift, a confused maintenance worker will find a cardboard box full of trash in the Blue Line tunnel. He'll never meet the woman who left it there and rejoined the world, unencumbered.

Coambulation

Elderly man—let's call him Carl—sporting slick bald scalp and thick white beard steps lively down busy city streets, black messenger bag bouncing happily on every stride against dodgy hip. Arms swing easy in empty air, nose sniffs ceaselessly to test blooming summer scents after sudden shower. Sleeveless, blue-red floral dress hangs over wrinkled, masculine shoulders, still strong; slightly frayed hem wafts, flutters just above worn leather combat boot tops.

Cheerful codger stops at boulevard corner crossing, doesn't take advantage of flashing green WALK—rather, removes rimless spectacles, lowers them while lifting flowing, flowery folds. Finely filed fingernails punctuate nimble digits: that cool coot tries wiping those Coke bottles clean. Quite obviously dissatisfied with results, holds left lens (followed by right) within cavernous mouth, makes raspy little sighing sound as fog forms. Extra moisture seems helpful, eliminates whatever oily mess had been blurring vision before. Granddad gives glasses one last polish, then slides goggles back onto face.

Pappy sets off once again, resumes place among urban bustle. Fellow pedestrians have begun noticing old four-eyes' presence, especially because: SOCIALLY UNACCEPTABLE WARDROBE CHOICE. Paces slow, gawkers turn torsos, sniggers sneak out, index fingers all around, hurtful words whispered behind palms, hushed scandal [for shame!], craning necks shoot sideways glances through car windows zooming past.

Our friendly geezer hears these barbs, keeps head aloft, smiles despite unwarranted cruelty. Do not pity his lot. Instead, consider this:

He sees more clearly than they ever will.

Dear Mother

Mother doesn't know, no, she doesn't.

Mother doesn't know what I have in the basement.

She knows lots of other things, yes. She knows how to trick the squirrels to make them come into the house. She knows that the city is poisoning the water with chemicals, they're trying to control us. She knows that those men, those men with shiny black shoes and hair too clean are coming to get us and that we have to hide, sometimes. Yes, sometimes we have to hide. She teaches me all the things. All I'll ever need to know, she tells me so. I love mother more than the moon and the stars and all the wonders of the universe.

Mother's lessons are everything I could ever ask for. They are all color and light and movement, that's how you hold the children's attention, yes. That's how they learn. When she was a girl, she had to learn with books, they made her do it. Books are too flat and boring, they're just no good for little brains. Too many words and numbers cage in those budding minds, it stunts their growth, stunts it for sure. It narrows those poor babies' vision, yes, very narrow.

Mother tells me not to think too much about father, god-damn him, he will get his in the end. She tells me about how she used to be a beautiful woman and how all the men wanted to fuck her. She tells me to stop biting my nails. She tells me about her other baby, the one she really wanted, the one who withered and died in her womb, yes, it did. She tells me how black it all was when the baby came out.

Mother has eyes in the back of her head, nothing ever surprises her. She wouldn't let that happen, can't be an ir-responsible parent, no way she's going to let them take her GODDAMN CHILD. She has to protect her baby, lots of danger, watchers, traps set up by strangers. They'd just love to take me away and put me in a home, they'd just love it. She knows, too, she's seen it happen over and over and over. She won't let anyone take me away from her, she won't let me be lonely or scared. She'll always be vigilant, yes, always vigilant for her little one's sake.

Mother gave me my hiding cloak last year, all mine. She spent three days making it, and she didn't sleep the whole time, no. It was all different materials and colors and stitches, and she put her sweat and blood into that thing, yes, she did. She said I had to wear it or the crows would see me, see what I did. The crows used to sit in the tree outside our house in the fall. Mother said they were always there but you could only see them when the leaves were all gone and the branch-es looked like skinny fingers, all bones. The cloak worked, because one day the crows didn't show up. They never came back again, never. Mother said they got tired of looking for me.

Mother brushes my hair and sings me songs that come to her in dreams. Sometimes the songs are warm and soft, but sometimes they are storms and cacophony, because that's life.

Mother says that honest songs are the best songs, yes, they are. She tells me my hair is more beautiful than spun gold. Mother would never lie.

Today is mother's birthday, yes, she is wearing her special gown. There's only one occasion to wear such a precious thing, don't you think that's true? Her hair is done up all in curls and it glitters like diamonds on a beach, wouldn't you agree? She glides across the floor like a starlet from the golden age of film, she's so glamorous. She sits at the head of the table, because this is her fucking household. She is ready for her gift now, the one she knows I've been working on, busy busy bee. I have to go get it mother, you wait here. I have to go get your pretty present. You wait here, mother, I'll be right back. The walls go whish by my face, the end of the hall. Mother is never surprised, no, not ever, but things change sometimes. Basement door, click-clack. She'll be so surprised, yes, I'm sure, it's so pretty. Down, down, down, all the stairs. How could she know? She can't possibly. I've kept it hidden, kept it in the spot she won't go to anymore. Yes, there it is, in its hidden spot, nice and hidey. No, she can't know what it is, can't know what it is at all.

Mother doesn't know what I have in the basement.

But she will soon.

Sweetness

The party was over, and visible currents of heat rose from the roof of the minivan. Black hadn't been the best color choice, but beggars can't be choosers. Maria had never been a chooser.

The car had cost about half as much as the next best option on the market, and it was a good little delivery vehicle apart from the scuffs and scrapes, most of which she had simply covered up with vinyl appliqués announcing:

Make Way for Royalty!
The Princess Confectioner:
Handmade Pastries and Sweets

She had initially written "confectionist" on the order form; she realized that it wasn't a real word only after she had rushed home from the print shop and frantically searched the Internet for businesses that might already be using that name. Thankfully, there was no risk of a lawsuit, and she was able to change her order before it went to print. She had also listed her cell number and web address on the van. The website was still aspirational; it had been a major blow to her confidence when her first attempt at setting it up looked nothing like the page she was trying to copy. The advertisement on the van didn't include a physical address at all, as she was still doing all the baking in the kitchen of her studio apartment; she figured she would be able to rent an actual storefront by the end of the year, assuming business picked up.

The little girl's mother had called late one evening and asked if Maria was available on the seventeenth. Maria had put on a skit in which she checked her busy schedule and said that she could probably move a few things around.

"Do you do macaroons?" the woman had asked. "My daughter had them at a friend's party last week and won't shut up about them."

"Of course," Maria said politely, adding, "Are you sure you don't mean *macarons*, though? They're much more popular than macaroons these days."

"I'm not a moron," the woman replied testily. "I need them dipped in chocolate. Can you do that?"

"I can do them any way you like, ma'am," Maria said, trying to ignore the sting in her throat until the deal was sealed. "How many do you need?"

The seventeenth arrived on schedule, and Maria had already been baking for several hours by the time the sun rose; three hundred macaroons were going to take the better part of eight hours to bake, and she wanted to have plenty of wiggle room before the party at two.

The wiggle came in handy at the guardhouse of the gated community. Maria wasn't on the list and had to wait almost twenty minutes while the guard tried to contact the girl's parents; the man in the booth finally reached the father and waved Maria through. It took her a further five minutes to reach the house on account of the ridiculous number of speed bumps in the neighborhood and the fact that the suspension on the van really wasn't up to the job. She drove at a snail's pace to protect the work she'd done in the kitchen and used the time to guess at what the appeal of living in such a contrived, detached place might be.

The question answered itself as she pulled into the clients' circuitous cobblestone driveway; the house that rose into view was larger than any she had ever seen, with a pair of matching Mercedes sparkling out front. After the sense of awe had worn off, she climbed the broad steps to the porch and found a note on the monolithic front door instructing her to enter and exit the property via the gate on the north side of the house; it also indicated that she was to park on the street so that guests could use the driveway. She checked which side of the house she needed to be on—this required some backtracking after an unlucky first try—before moving the van to the curb.

Balancing too many trays on her knee and wondering how many more trips she would have to make back to the street, Maria managed to get the side gate open. She was greeted almost immediately by the birthday girl's father, who apologized for the confusion at the guardhouse and offered to take some of the trays before leading her to the table where she was supposed to set up. She had more than enough space for her arrangement at the base of an expertly carved ice sculpture of what she could only assume was the birthday girl's face. After a few trips back to the van and quite a bit of fiddling, Maria felt she could be proud of the spread she had prepared. She looked up just in time to see the girl's mother coming out onto the patio through the French doors at the rear of the house.

"What the hell are these?" the woman demanded, her pace quickening and shoulders hunching has she approached the table.

"Chocolate-dipped macaroons, as requested," Maria said, her pride suddenly replaced with concern.

"This isn't what I ordered," the woman said, wrinkling her nose as she sniffed at one of the confections. "Is this coconut?"

"Yes, ma'am," Maria replied evenly, "macaroons are traditionally made with coconut and almonds."

"What kind of kid likes coconut?" the woman asked derisively. "Why didn't you make what I asked for?"

"I tried to clarify that with you on the phone, ma'am," Maria said, struggling to stay civil. "You assured me you knew the difference."

"Oh, no you don't," the woman said, tossing the macaroon down and wagging a finger in Maria's face. "You're not going to pin your fuck-up on me. I was perfectly clear about what I wanted. Now, get this crap out of here. Harold, run over to Dennigan's—I'm going to call in a rush order of cupcakes."

The girl's mother stormed back into the house without any further acknowledgment of Maria's presence; the father caught up to Maria as she was exiting through the side gate. He mumbled something about excusing his wife as he tucked a folded check into the pocket of her apron; the back of his hand lingered against her thigh just long enough to raise questions. He and Maria avoided eye contact when she returned for the second batch of trays, and again when she saw him driving toward the street as she walked back up the driveway to retrieve the last of her things.

Wincing under the oppression of summer sun and dripping with frustration, Maria stared at the sheets of uneaten pastries stacked neatly in the back of a van whose dents had become obvious and scratches apparent. It was a wholly insufficient thing, she saw, and she was an idiot for having bought it. How had she not realized that people had been laughing at her, snickering as she bustled around trying to impress? She was a fool for coming, for thinking this stupid business would work in the first place. She was a fool for thinking these people would treat her with dignity. She was a fool.

She rummaged around blindly in her apron pocket for the check the girl's father had put there, but the folded slip of paper was nowhere to be found. Instead, a cool, hard, slick something insinuated itself into her palm.

"What the hell?" she whispered, frowning at the inexplicable ice pick in her hand.

"*Don't tell me you don't recognize me,*" a voice chortled from behind her.

She whirled around to see who had spoken the words, but there wasn't anybody there.

"*Look a little closer to home, dear,*" the voice chuckled, this time from a place between her ears.

"Who are you? What is this?" Maria nearly shouted, panic scrambling up her legs.

"*I'm your self-respect, you imbecile,*" the voice giggled; the sharp little puppet in her hand danced a jig to the rhythm of the words in her head. "*Aww, what's wrong, dummy? Cat got your tongue?*" the voice mocked when Maria managed nothing more than a confused half-utterance. "*Fine, I'll do the talking. I wasn't all that interested in hearing what you had to say, anyway. Here's the deal: I'm tired of being stuck on the sidelines while you let every asshole and cunt in the world walk all over us. Until you start doing your job, I'll be calling the shots. Nod to let me know you understand, please.*"

Maria felt something burrow into her hair and clench tightly; her head was wrenched back and then thrown forward.

"*Wonderful,*" the voice tinkled. "*Now, you're sorely mistaken if you think I'm going to let you swallow this one, honey. Little Miss Birthday Bitch needs to learn how to play nice. Luckily, I know just how to handle the situation.*"

It took a while, and Maria left a few fingernails tucked under the arms of the windshield wipers during the struggle, but the three police officers finally succeeded in pulling her down from the hood of the Mercedes. The vehicle's body panels had been thoroughly aerated, and its tires puddled under the wheels; cubic shards of the driver's side window glittered in the stuffing of the disemboweled leather interior, which in turn was soaking up the melted remains of several dozen macaroons. The car's owner had finally stopped screaming; she wore a look of bewilderment, thrown into glistening relief by the ropey mass of phlegm Maria had plastered across the right side of her face.

Maria didn't say a word as the cops guided her into the back seat of the cruiser and ran her shackles through a steel loop welded to the floor; she merely smiled quietly to herself as they pulled away, a dented attempt at happiness shrinking into oblivion behind her.

Worms

A long, long time ago, people did not eat worms. One of those people was a man named Lethabo.

One morning before dawn, Lethabo set out from his village to fetch a sack of corn porridge from the nearest town. His family had not eaten in three days, and they were very hungry. Even though they did not like corn porridge, they could hardly wait for him to return.

The town was far away from the village, and Lethabo walked quickly so that he could return before nightfall. Walking quickly was not something that people from his village usually did, but he knew how hungry his family was, and he did not want them to suffer any longer. However, he did not let the fact that he was in a hurry make him forget his manners.

"Good morning, Sun," Lethabo said to the slice of light peeking over the northern mountains. "Thank you for giving us warmth and helping us to see."

"Good morning, Lethabo," Sun said. "Here, I will help you see the way to the town."

Lethabo was very thankful for Sun's help, but by the time he reached the town, he wished Sun had been a little less helpful. Lethabo was covered in sweat, and his feet were blistered and sore from walking on the hot ground. Of course, he was too polite to ask Sun to go away, so he just tried to find some shade as soon as he could.

"The streets of the town are very empty today," Lethabo thought as he approached the market square. He did not give it any more thought, though, because his feet hurt so very much and his hunger was becoming too much to bear.

"You are a brave man to be outside on a day like this," the grain merchant said as he handed a sack of corn porridge to Lethabo and peered through the granary's only window. "I wish you luck."

"Thank you very much," Lethabo replied, thinking the man was talking about the sweltering journey back to the village.

Very soon, he found out what the man had actually meant.

Lethabo was nearing the town gate when they appeared from around the corner of a nearby tin shack: the girls walked all in a row, shaved heads lowered and swaying, arms held still at their sides and long grass skirts swishing as they went. They wore nothing else except for the reddish clay that had been smeared all over their skin. At the end of the long chain of girls was their matron: Mama Langa, wide as she was tall—and she was very tall, indeed—beating the rhythm of the march in the dirt with the hefty length of acacia she carried with her.

Lethabo knew that men were not allowed to witness the girls' rite of passage, and he felt foolish for having forgotten that it was the day of the ritual. He did not have long to feel foolish, though, because he could see that Mama Langa had stopped marching and was staring directly at him.

"Aaaiiieeeee!" Mama Langa screamed as she raised her baton and charged at Lethabo.

"Aaaaaaaaah!" screamed Lethabo, clutching his porridge sack tightly as he ran for the gate.

Lethabo ran and ran across the fields that surrounded the town, which had been newly threshed in the harvest. He soon reached the far edge of the farmed land, where a wall of tall grass rose up in front of him like an ocean. When he turned around, he could see that the town was just a speck in the distance. Mama Langa was a larger speck—one that was getting larger all the time—so he pushed into the green waves and started running again, as best he could.

Running through the hip-high grass was very tiring for Lethabo, especially with Sun helping as much as he still was. He knew that Mama Langa would run in his wake when she reached the grassy sea, which would help her catch up even more quickly. He could see no way out of his predicament and had almost given up hope when he saw Rabbit nibbling on a blade of grass nearby.

"Rabbit!" Lethabo cried. "Please, help me! The grass is too tall, and Mama Langa is coming. If she catches me, she will surely beat me!"

"Come!" said Rabbit. "I will let you crawl through my burrow. Mama Langa cannot fit inside!"

Lethabo followed Rabbit until they reached a hole in the ground that was just big enough for Lethabo to enter. He began to climb in after Rabbit, but his porridge sack was much too full to fit into the confined space. It saddened him to have to pour some of the corn porridge out, but he knew it was better than what Mama Langa had in store for him.

When the two reached the other end of the cramped tunnel, Lethabo saw that they had come out beyond the sea of grass. He did not know exactly where he was, and he was eager to escape back to his village, but he made sure to express his gratitude before continuing on his way.

"Many thanks, Rabbit," Lethabo said as he stretched his legs. "I will do my best to repay you someday!"

As the grasslands disappeared behind him, Lethabo wished that he could slow down and catch his breath for a while, but Mama Langa's speck was once again growing on the horizon. Much to his dismay, he was forced to stop entirely when he reached a wall of brambles that stretched as far as he could see in either direction. The vines were very dense, and it hurt to even look at their long, sharp thorns. Lethabo paced back and forth, trying to stay calm and thinking about what he could possibly do next. Nothing came to him. Just when he was about to lie down and wait for Mama Langa to arrive, he saw Snake slither out from the depths of the thorny blockade.

"Snake!" Lethabo pleaded. "Please, help me find a way to escape! Mama Langa is coming for me!"

"Come!" Snake replied. "I will show you a path through the brush. Crawl on your belly like I do!"

Lethabo did as snake instructed, wriggling on his belly along a hidden passage through the spiny vines. He felt his worry leave him as he crawled, but the celebration was cut short when he noticed that the brambles were tearing lots of little holes in his porridge sack. His corn porridge spilled out little by little as he progressed, and because he could not do anything about it for fear of being jabbed by the thorns, his sack was mostly empty by the time he and Snake reached the other side. He was very upset about the porridge, and he did not want to give Mama Langa any more time to catch up to him, but he did not let his anxiety make him run off before thanking Snake.

"I owe you a debt, my friend," Lethabo said, rearranging his sack to stop the last of the porridge from spilling out. "I promise, I will return the favor somehow!"

With the brambles little more than a memory, Lethabo ran across an expanse of scrubby pasture until he came to a fence that the local goatherds had built. It was much too tall for him to climb, and just like the brambles before it, it was so long that he could not see the ends. He could, however, see Mama Langa in the distance once again. Fearing that this might be the end of his journey, he had begun to practice his surrender when he happened to see Antelope grazing nearby.

"Antelope!" Lethabo called. "Please, can you help me? Mama Langa is coming, and I need to get through!"

"Come!" said Antelope. "I will show you the lowest part of the fence. You can jump over, like I do!"

When they reached the dip in the fence, Lethabo jumped the way Antelope showed him. He could not jump as well as Antelope, but he managed to clear the fence without hurting himself. Unfortunately, his sack of corn porridge snagged on a fencepost on the way down, and everything that was left in the sack spilled onto the ground. Lethabo was very perturbed at this, but still he did not forget his manners.

"Thank you, dear friend," he said, bowing slightly. "I will not forget your kindness!"

Clutching his empty porridge sack as he ran off, Lethabo soon realized why the herdsmen had built the fence. The desert that stretched out in front of him was no place for goats—or anyone else, for that matter. There was no grass. There were no brambles or fences. There was not anything except for Sun, miles and miles of hard-baked ground, and a very old-looking mopani tree in the distance.

Sun was being more helpful than he had ever been, and though Lethabo tried to use his empty sack as a hat, he was so hot that sweat poured from the tip of his nose and evaporated before it hit the ground. He eventually made it to the mopani tree, but by that time his legs were so tired that he could barely stand. He collapsed in a heap in the shade of the tree and looked up to see Worm and a few hundred of his brothers sitting in its branches.

"Worm!" Lethabo called in a parched voice. "Please, help me! I can run no more, and Mama Langa is almost here!"

However, Worm did not reply. He and his brothers simply continued crawling very slowly along the branches of the mopani tree and munching on its leaves.

Lethabo's time had come, and before he knew it, Mama Langa was standing over him. Her legs were stained the color of grass, there were brambles wrapped around her waist and tearing holes in her dress, and she was carrying a large chunk of broken fencepost in her teeth. She was also carrying Lethabo's friends Rabbit, Snake, and Antelope clutched in one powerful hand. In the other hand, she held her trusty acacia branch, which she raised over her head without saying a word.

Lethabo lost count of how many times Mama Langa hit him over the head, but when he finally opened his eyes again, he could see her peering down at him in what proved to be a very deep, Lethabo-shaped pit at the foot of the mopani tree. She threw his friends in after him and, after snorting loudly, started walking back in the direction of the town.

"Why are you here, my friends?" Lethabo asked the others as Mama Langa's earth-shaking footsteps grew quieter. "Did you see the girls' ritual, too?"

"Mama Langa was not happy that we helped you," said Rabbit, massaging the twist out of his ears with his paw.

"She tore the brambles out by the roots to get to me," said Snake, who was trying his best to undo the knot in his tail.

"The fence is no more," said Antelope as he licked the bruises on his hind legs. "Also, I did not think someone so large could move so quickly."

"I am sorry I brought this upon you, but now it is my turn to help you all," Lethabo said, smiling at his friends. "I have an idea."

He told the others his plan, and they all agreed that it was a very good one.

First, Lethabo let Antelope stand on his back.

"Jump, Antelope!" he shouted, and Antelope jumped clear out of the hole.

"Now it is your turn, Snake," Lethabo said. He picked up his legless friend and threw him out of the pit.

"Rabbit, climb!" Lethabo exclaimed, and Rabbit pulled himself along Snake's body, which was secured at one end to Antelope's horns. Lethabo was too heavy to climb out as Rabbit had, but he had already thought about that.

"Now, all three of you—shake the tree!" he called.

His friends did as he had said, and soon Worm and his brothers began to fall from the branches and into the pit.

"Yes, good!" Lethabo cheered. "Keep shaking!"

Before long, the pit was so full of worms that Lethabo was able to climb right out. The four friends were glad to be free, and they congratulated each other on a job well done.

At last, Lethabo no longer had to fear Mama Langa's wrath, and he could finish his journey home in peace. He wished his friends good luck and safe travels, and then he turned back to the pit and began stuffing his porridge sack full of worms.

"What are you doing, Lethabo?" the confused animals asked in unison.

"Well," Lethabo replied as he broke into a smile, "I can't return to my family empty-handed, can I?"

Fame Beast

Kit's cigarette flares as he sucks on it, nicotine and tar tanning the back of his throat. He watches the end of the Lucky Strike necrotize until it can't support its own weight anymore, and something inside him jumps every time the corpsed portion falls onto the pile he's started on the virgin leather of the couch. The feeling doesn't extend to Casey's monologue, which Kit wishes would just end already. Her voice is taking on a thrilled kind of breathiness as she paces around the living room and rearranges furniture while recounting the earlier happenings at Nieman's.

"I try them on, and they fit perfectly, but then when I go to walk around in them, the right heel just snaps and nearly kills me," Casey says, acting out the stumble. "It definitely wasn't me—you know I'm on the eighth day of my cleanse, so I'm down like fifteen pounds. Anyway, I bend down to take them off before I completely eat shit, and the sales girl runs over and gets these giant footprints all over the bottom of my dress. That thing was *gorgeous*, and she totally ruined it. The manager chewed her out in front of everyone in the store. I bet she's going to get fired."

"No, I get it," Kit says without diverting his gaze from the growing pile of white-gray soot at the edge of the armrest. "Couldn't you have said something to help her out though, Case? Nothing actually happened to you, and I bought you that dress. I can just buy you another one." He cantilevers the char out a bit farther as he thinks about the peculiarities of having this or that kind of genitalia. He wonders if there is some evolutionary benefit to being cruel.

"Whatever," Casey snorts with a handwave. "She should have thought about that before she went and destroyed my dress with her monster feet. Anyway, the store comped me all this shit," she says as she looks down at her outfit, scarecrow elbows ascendant. "I think this skirt makes my ass look hot. Look at that."

"Yep. Hot," Kit offers halfheartedly. "Hey, you want an espresso? I'm dragging."

Casey's hair lashes out at the non sequitur, but Kit doesn't notice. He hauls himself off the couch, opting for hands and knees before climbing to his feet. *Hit it a little too hard last night*, he thinks, not for the first time this week.

Casey fishes her cell phone out of her clutch, holding it in one hand while she tries to untangle her headphones with the other. Kit has shown her a trick for winding the cord to make it tangle-proof, but she looks to have returned to the old stuff-and-snarl technique. He watches her struggle and wonders if a second demonstration would take. She and Kit are screwing, but neither of them is interested in putting a label on what they have, or really committing to anything at all. She's happy to be banging a celebrity and living rent-free, and he's fine with not having to pay cash for sex or brave the outside world to find someone new.

Kit's bare feet slap softly against architectural concrete as he crosses a scandal's worth of unused square footage on his way to the kitchen, where a mountain of serpentine stainless steel and thick handles perches on the center island. Kit doesn't actually like the taste of coffee, but he can't get enough of the smell. It reminds him of when he used to be able to go out to places like coffee shops and restaurants without giving it a second thought. Getting that aroma just right was worth spending as much as he did on the commercial-grade setup, which he knows was more than anyone in their right mind would have. He really wishes he could stomach the stuff; it's always struck him as funny that cocaine plays well enough with his system, but that something as mundane as coffee always turns him into a miserable mess of jitters. For what it's worth, both make him have to shit when he doesn't want to.

He pulls out a container of his favorite blend and turns to ask Casey if she wants any milk or sugar, only to catch a fleeting glimpse of the back of her headphoned head leaving the room. He knows that if he wants to be heard, he'll have to chase her down. His feet flex, but then they relax as he decides his energy is better spent playing barista for one.

Staring down into a cold, half-empty cup of coffee about an hour later, Kit toys with the idea of overcoming his inertia and going out, but there are always so many goddamn paparazzi waiting outside the house that even the thought of it makes him flinch. He took a swing at one of them a few months ago and had to issue a public apology, which he found pretty galling considering the punch hadn't even connected. He concludes that it's much too early and sober to deal with the hyenas just yet, but he thinks he might be able to run the gauntlet to get to the gallery opening tonight. He doesn't know the featured artist—personally or by reputation—but his agent told him it would be a good way to keep his face in the public eye, seeing as he didn't put out a record last year. Checking the time bums him out: he still has six hours to kill before he can leave for the gala, and that's if he wants to be the first to arrive. So, he has about seven and a half hours to kill.

He smokes a bowl to pass some time, but paranoia sets in before he's able to enjoy himself. His feelings of overexposure get on top of him, and he spends the next two hours curtain-twitching and evading the view of the binocular-toting stalkers he knows are out there. Doing tai-chi in the mansion's windowless basement gym while Rachmaninoff blares over the stereo proves helpful in pulling him back from the edge.

When he finally comes down from the high, it's almost time for him to leave for the gallery. He wants to ask Casey to come with him, but based on her frequent proclamations that she "doesn't get art" and the way she behaved at the last function to which he took her, he decides to leave her in peace. Despite his earlier optimism, he isn't prepared to deal with the gutter press waiting beyond the gates; he calls for a car, emphasizing the need for blackout windows. Fifteen minutes later, Glenn buzzes up from the gatehouse to inform him that his ride has arrived.

At the gallery, Kit does his best chameleon impression and tries to take in some culture, but the after-effects of the weed are making it difficult to pay attention to any one thing for very long.

"You seem pretty fixated—are you a fan of his work?" one woman asks, breaking Kit's focus on a floor-to-ceiling self-portrait of the evening's host. It turns out the woman is speaking to her friend.

"Oh, no. Not really," the friend says, checking around her to make sure the subject of their discussion isn't within earshot. "I just think it's intriguing that *he's* so fixated. On what others think of him, you know? I actually think his work is a little juvenile. I guess the two go hand in hand."

Kit's subsequent analysis of a sintered bronze sculpture is interrupted by a bohemian couple's delineation of the latest tragedy on the far end of the world.

"Wasn't that video heartbreaking?" the wisp of a girl says to her other half, who seems to be more interested in a passing tray of canapés than the sculpture in front of him. "I can't imagine having my life upended like that."

"Yeah, I guess," he says, his attention having drifted back to his wife. "But really, look at those people—they looked like that before the typhoon. The typhoon didn't make them unfortunate."

Studying a performance piece involving a nude, nongendered model inserting various children's toys into alternating nostrils, Kit has almost put his finger on the intended symbolism when a voice knocks him off the path to enlightenment; Devon, an A-List celebrity whom Kit has heard referred to as a fashion icon—and nothing else—is brow-beating a man who Kit is fairly sure works in the magazine business and is named Lemar.

"Well, then maybe that person should become a critic," Devon jeers at Lemar, referring to something Kit must have missed, "and maybe that person is a worthless sack of shit who invites himself to parties and who no one wants to be around."

Lemar stands there for a few stunned seconds, during which Devon turns back to address his hangers-on.

"Hey, man, that was—that was harsh," Lemar finally sputters. "You really took it over the line, man."

"*JE-sus*. Is anyone still talking to you?" Devon nearly yells, looking briefly at the ceiling before glaring at Lemar again. "Fuck off, *man*."

Later, Kit hugs the wall near the champagne fountain and tries to tune out the thinly veiled self-promotion going on nearby.

"Are you coming to my opening next week, dear?" Henrika—just *Henrika*—asks a turtlenecked man who is trying to make his exit from the group. "It won't be as lavish as all this, but you know me. No accounting for taste." They blow air kisses to one another before Henrika continues. "Now, where were we? Oh, yes—I know it's vain. It's completely narcissistic, I know that. There are some people who absolutely have the right to make everyone else see the world through their eyes, disadvantaged people that the privileged minority forgets about. I'm not one of those people, and I'm very aware of the fact that I've usurped that right, but I do think the way I see the world is special. It might not be, but good luck getting me to change the habit, especially when people keep paying the kind of money they do for my work."

Kit reaches his limit sometime around one and heads for the coat check. As he tips the attendant and shimmies into his jacket, he can't help overhearing the heated conversation going on in the adjoining hall.

"It was well written, absolutely," says a woman with tortured diction. "I just thought the film was a little too cynical."

"Too cynical?" a male voice guffaws. "Have you ever been to Africa? Look, it's great that things are all roses and sunshine for you, but life is a dark fucking thing for most people."

When Kit gets home, he searches the mansion for Casey, who is nowhere to be found. The Bentley is gone, and Kit's Japanese cigarette case is missing from its place on the coffee table, so he has a hunch as to where she might have gone. He isn't worried about her—she knows how to handle herself with the coke—but he knows he likely won't see her until tomorrow afternoon at the earliest.

Back on the couch, Kit chases a handful of pills with a few swallows of vodka and makes a wager with himself about how long the blackout will be in coming. He flips on the TV and tries to find something worth watching, only to be met with entertainment journalists daring to ask the burning questions that no one should have to bother answering. When he finally sees that there is no other way, he relents and prostrates himself before the Moloch squatting on every channel; his piety is rewarded with a regurgitated stream of moments he didn't realize had been stolen from his life, twisted in a high-definition funhouse mirror. Night dissolves around him, and he feels himself growing thinner as the weak light of morning presses against the drawn shades. Just before he loses consciousness, his thumb makes one last, frenzied attempt on the channel button of the remote.

Nothing changes.

The Juggler

AMAZING. ASTOUNDING. FEARLESS.
COME SEE THE WORLD'S MOST
DEATH-DEFYING SPECTACLE!

The words jumped from the paper, jarring white against a dark blue background. Kalos Thanolaki's glinting eyes and winning smile beamed out from the poster's hyperreal tableau, variegated primary colors printed slightly off-center. Kalos was pictured with his signature handlebar mustache and well-kempt helm of coal-black hair, swept back and frozen in place with pomade and photographic immortality. The horizontal stripes of his singlet strained to cover the herculean breadth of his chest, while the tree trunks above his knees stretched fabric to its limit.

The circus was using these posters—"classic" was the term Kalos had heard the boss use—to try to drum up some more business, hoping that a shot of nostalgia would prompt older folks to bring their kids or grandkids to the big show on the weekends. Kalos was unsure whether the new posters would be enough to turn the tide; the crowds had been thinning for years. There had been one noteworthy spike in attendance three years prior, in the wake of Pietro's accidental death. The acrobat had missed the landing on his high-wire double front flip and plummeted the forty feet down from the trapeze. Pietro had been famous for performing his feats of daring without a safety net. Well, thought Kalos, he was still famous for that, just in a slightly different context than before.

At first, the circus folk were appalled by the morbid curiosity which drove ticket sales, but that sensitivity soon faded as cash loaded the coffers and applause filled the performers' ears. Sadly, the renaissance lasted little more than two months—when no one else died during the show, the people just seemed to lose interest again. The ensuing trickle of attrition quickly rose to break the levee, and soon the outfit was back to just barely scraping by.

Kalos had never minded the smaller crowds. In his world, the night had been a success so long as he had managed to entertain a single person. Each time he performed, he would make note of one lucky spectator and make sure that he thrilled them at least once during his act. He'd yet to have gone to bed doubting.

Apart from Grandma Gillie, Kalos had been performing longer than anyone else in the show. His was a rare double act called the Gladiator's Inferno, in which Kalos would juggle four flaming swords while wrestling his best friend, Attila, who also happened to be the circus's lion. As was the case with all lions in his line of work, Attila had been declawed as a cub to minimize the threat he could pose, but the audience didn't need to know that. Kalos never let Attila get the upper hand, anyway. They had an understanding that if Kalos were made to look like a fool during the show, Attila would not get his treat—typically a bucket of bartered offal from the local butcher shop—when the two retired to their shared wagon after the show. Attila was very partial to his treats; Kalos remained a fool unmade.

Attila, consummate entertainer though he was, had begun to grow long of tooth and gray of mane. Kalos had his own fair share of lines in his face and silvery hairs in his beard, but time had been unequivocally harsher to his feline companion. One would have been right to forgive Attila his somewhat ragged appearance: the big cat had already seen fifteen years, a feat that few lions—captive or wild—ever manage. Though it felt like the two had been together for ages, Attila was actually the second lion with whom Kalos had worked. The first had been brought on ten years into Kalos's career—then, as with the posters now, to give the show's flagging attendance a shot in the arm.

That lion was Goliath, who had been purchased from a zoo which had been forced to close due to animal welfare concerns. The circumstances had thrown up a red flag in Kalos's mind at the time, but he was already accustomed to doing what he was told and keeping his head down, so his concerns had gone unvoiced. The other performers had told Kalos not to agree to do the new act; they had told him that beasts in the show needed to be brought up in the show. Animal acts always had an element of unpredictability, even under the best conditions, and Goliath had certainly not come to them under those.

Emaciated and distrustful upon his arrival, Goliath was unapproachable for his first two weeks in residence. Kalos had volunteered for the duties involved with Goliath's care—he'd figured that the quickest way to gain the lion's trust was to become the Hand that Feeds. The two were able to establish a tenuous working arrangement, but after five years of not entirely trusting one another, their relationship took an unfortunate turn when Goliath very nearly took off Kalos's right hand during the act one night. Kalos had been able to conceal the bite wound until the next act drew the audience's attention, but the stitches his hand had required and the subsequent recuperation had put him out of the show for several very painful months. In the aftermath of the ordeal, Kalos had finally found his voice and informed the boss that he would no longer be performing as long as Goliath was still part of the show. The boss was a loyal man, and he agreed on the spot; Goliath was sold to the next taker, who in this case had been a sheik who was expanding his menagerie and who had paid, in cash, almost twice what the lion was worth. Kalos was not sad to see the cat go.

Attila the Cub had been acquired from another circus operation over on the coast. That show had included a pair of lions who had gone about demonstrating their disdain for statistics by enthusiastically reproducing in captivity. Kalos's boss had gotten wind of the development well in advance, and had been first in line when the female birthed her litter. Attila and Kalos had been inseparable ever since.

Before heading back to the tent to practice, Kalos took one last look at the new-old poster. Attila definitely wasn't as lithe and powerful as pictured anymore, but that light in his eyes remained. The two had a lot of good years behind them; Kalos tried not to worry about the precious few ahead.

The night's audience was marginally larger than the night before's. Though it was likely too soon to call the new ad campaign a success, Kalos decided that tempered optimism wasn't unwarranted. The cast certainly did their best to earn the crowd's admiration: the Romatti twins were in fine form, garnering healthy applause for their high-flying antics, despite the use of a net. Gonzo and his motley troupe of clowns made a perfectly choreographed mess of themselves to the sound of riotous laughter. Madame Gouland and Trixie, her gorgeous young Appaloosa, dazzled as they raced around the center ring.

As Kalos watched his compatriots do what they did best, his eyes were suddenly drawn to a small face in the crowd. It belonged to a ruddy-haired boy, no older than ten, who was sitting perfectly still in the space between his parents and wearing the most bored expression Kalos had ever seen. A hint of interest flared briefly in the boy's dull eyes when Trixie faltered, but it subsided as soon as it became clear that Madame Gouland wasn't going to be thrown out of her handstand. None of the other performances seemed to register with the boy in the least.

Kalos and Attila's act was the show's finale; if anything were going to stir the young visitor's interest, it would be the Inferno. The lion and the strongman rushed into the ring, and the tent billowed with thunderous applause. Swords were doused in flame, teeth were borne, and muscles were flexed to their limits in pantomime mortal combat. Between catching burning swords, fending off Attila's feigned rancor, and mugging for the audience, Kalos scanned the crowd for the Unamused One. When he finally found him, he realized the boy was not watching the show at all, but rather pulling testily on his father's sleeve and pointing toward the exit.

Undeterred, Kalos resorted to more drastic measures, which in this case meant dusting off the Burning King. The act involved the addition of a fifth sword and Kalos riding around on the back of his subservient foe, and it had been years since the duo had attempted it. Kalos gave the signal, but Attila balked at the command, clearly incensed by his friend's disregard for his advanced age and the dignity it should have entailed. He obeyed the second time, though, likely having remembered the threat of having to forgo his tasty treats.

The King, while a mere shadow of its former self, was still spectacular. Kalos even landed the dismount from Attila's back, though a bite of pain indicated that he had probably sprained his ankle in the process. Swimming in whistles and whoops and beaming victory, Kalos swung around to see the look on the face of his newest fan. Three empty seats stared back at him.

The show was over; Kalos lingered only long enough for his comrades to join him in the ring for the final bow. The roar of the crowd undoubtedly signaled to the others that the night had been a triumph, but all Kalos could hear was the one small silence. He excused himself from the post-performance revelry, citing his ankle and a sudden sleepiness before gingerly following Attila out through the tent's southern exit.

The two carried out their evening ritual back at the wagon, with costumes stowed carefully away, bucketed innards offered in the corner, and bedding of two sorts laid out next to each other; there was a lack of luster to the proceedings that Kalos knew they both felt. The friends belly-flopped into their respective beds, and Kalos let his right arm dangle over the side of the thin mattress so he could pet Attila as he always did: running a gently cupped palm over the lion's snout and forehead, grabbing a handful of hair just aft of the ears to give his massive head a little shake, then relaxing his grip and finishing with a sweep down the neck and shoulders.

Kalos's hand drifted to a halt as his mind returned to the boy's dispassionate face staring out from the dimmed grandstand. He imagined the whole world falling into that empty gaze, and an unfamiliar sensation crept into his brain; it gave the unpleasant impression of pulling on the backs of his eyeballs and made him feel as if he were standing on something narrow in a very high place.

A moist nudge against the edge his hand brought him back to his senses. As Kalos resumed petting his insistent companion, the alien feeling seeped down through the strongman's neck and shoulder, pulling heavily along the exhausted sinew in his arm. Some time later, the last of it squeezed through his wrist and left his body by way of his fingertips, evaporating into warm nothingness in the silver tangle of Attila's mane.

The Ballad of Ful Gray

The air crackled with cinder as restless flames rose from the storyfire, a thin coil of smoke pooling against the roundhouse ceiling before snaking out through the thatch. The faces that surrounded the pit were cast in copper; a throng of nodding mothers, shocks of iridescent feathers performing the evening's prologue in the haze above their heads, did not notice the young boy who slipped past them to crowd in with his friends near the front. Reed shirts rustled and scraped as the boys jockeyed for the best view of what was to come.

The Teller emerged, as if poured, from the confines of a woven sedan chair. Her movements were those of a crane: delicate yet deliberate strides which carried her through the parting masses and into the dusty ring which surrounded the fire. She was, as had been all other Tellers before her, a mistress of the moon; ancient law proclaimed that only those touched by neither man nor sun were fit to carry the mysteries of the tribe.

The woman's phantasmal skin shone through with flickering light as she circled the pit three times, dragging a broom of braided lavender in the dirt behind her as she went. When the third revolution was through, her hands disappeared into the sleeves of her long linen robes, emerging a moment later as fists. These she opened over the fire, which responded in loudly hissing green. The villagers looked on in asphyxiated suspense as the flames licked hungrily between her slender fingers. Their silence lifted the Teller's voice to booming as she threw her hands to the heavens and sang:

> "Ye gathered here would hear the tale of one who lost his way, who wanders still through black of night to seek the light of day. Though I, and my part humble be, shall try not to offend, I cannot swear that all will dare to listen to the end.
>
> Though born of godly parentage, he was no favorite son: Ful Gray, the Ghost, was cast away, his birthright thus undone. The wood nymphs found him where he lay and raised him as their own; they taught him how to speak to trees and coax the life from stone.
>
> A vision of his father's face was all that he could see when every night he dreamed of doom and sought in vain to flee. His spritely keepers cooled his brow to ease his fevered mind; he woke each morn to weighty pangs of longing left behind.
>
> The years marched on and longing aged to anger in its turn, and anger then to wrath and wish to watch his father burn. The dryads did their best to calm and help him find his peace, but kindness could not stem the tide of rage that wouldn't cease.

So Ful the Gray did kneel and pray to gods he did not know; he begged them bitterly to teach to him how to overthrow the monster who had dared to leave his son to starve and die without compassion or the grace to give the reason why.

And when the god of conflagration harkened to his prayer, he learned the words to conjure fire out of the naked air. He thanked the spirit for the means to make the traitor pay and made a solemn oath that he would not be led astray.

With fervor and a zeal unbound the Ghost did train his craft, and when he saw the world ignite and turn to ash, he laughed. He plumbed the depths of darkness to reveal the spells of old, and burning hate drove hard his hand until his heart grew cold.

It was a night of starless sky he bade the woods farewell to seek the storied cave where his progenitor should dwell. With hunger more than man may have or wasting creature wild, he'd hunt the one who shunned him so when he was but a child.

So set Ful forth to scour the earth and hone his deadly art; he swore he'd find his father, fiend, and crush his living heart. His mother he would save from certain slavery and woe, and pardon her inaction all those many years ago.

Through countless lands his feet did fall and leave a furrowed trail; he found no hindrance high or deep enough to make him fail. He bested icy mountain passes and the frothing sea, then crossed the scorching desert sands with steadfast bravery.

At last did he discover there, beyond the land of thirst, the cavern that had been his fleeting quarry from the first. The signs of his heredity reached nearly to his chin—the bones about the grotto's mouth betrayed the beast within.

The rancid mist that left the place was feculent and sour, but such a trifle held no sway in that most crucial hour. Ful steeled himself and strode ahead into the hollow space, and going in he felt the wind blow warm upon his face.

He let himself be led by currents in the brackish air and reached an ancient fireplace encased beneath a stair. The blaze that roared before him was like none he'd ever known; he found his forebear by the hearth, decaying on the throne.

As Ful beheld his father's frame—a husk as old as time—the Gray God clambered from his seat and struck the mystic chime which hung around his narrow neck and shone as did the dawn; it sowed his sallow skin with rose and filled his form with brawn.

Such violent handsome youth returned as Gul the Gray grew straight that Ful, for shock, almost forgot his everlasting hate. The flawless figure shattered and began to bulge and twist; when it was done the Ghostly One could fit inside its fist.

The hulking gore that once was Gul loomed o'er his cheated ward, who fashioned tongues of summoned flame into a shining sword. Their thickened blood ran itching, searing, screaming in their veins, and each was eager to rejoice at combat's cold remains.

The echoes of their mighty clench rang rampant in the hall; Lord Gul, immortal strength unleashed, pinned Ful against the wall. Though sorely stunned, the Ghost could see—unless his time was past—that to prevail he must assail the hand that held him fast.

A swift and stunning flash of pain crashed up the creature's arm; the sword had sundered clean his hand and cauterized the harm. He cowered then and held aloft in shrinking, pleading shame the charm he'd worn: a penance to the one who bore his name.

The gift that fell from Gul Gray's hand was not enough to quell the Ghost of Fire's long-held desire to send his sire to hell. Ful tore to him the talisman and offered then in trade into his father's bare-laid breast the stillness of his blade.

The line of Gray was severed short as father fell to son; the Ghost was gladdened by the gash his patricide had done. He donned the treasure, now his own, and hastened to ascend the jagged stair up to the lair which held his labor's end.

But when he found his mother there behind the veil of gold, he could not have foreseen the news that he would soon be told: that Mother Gray had been the one who left him in the wood, and she would do it all again, and gladly, if she could.

For Ful was born not of her womb but of some human whore whom Gul beguiled with godly wiles and mounted on the moor. She whelped a mongrel in the mud, fair-skinned and dark of hair—the goddess, seething spite, decreed he'd never be her heir.

The babe was taken while he slept and spirited afield; he did not see his captor's glee to think his fate was sealed. She found a forest valley where there was no one to pry: a dim and disremembered copse where she could watch him die.

The crooked knife she hefted filled with hexes as she spoke; alas, the blade was somehow stayed before the killing stroke. Some blest enchantment seemed intent to shelter and to save, though she could clearly see the woods were lonely as a grave.

That muted magic kept the queen from lifting Gray again, and so she left him lying there and fled the phantom glen. It pained her not to be the one who culled the bastard boy, but knowing he would wither filled her wicked heart with joy.

And when the witch's tale was done, Ful felt his fury bloom; he grabbed the harpy by the hair and dragged her from the room. Her body buckled as he bowled her down the corridor; she kicked and shrieked as her blood streaked across the fetid floor.

Gray did not deign to slack his grip once they had left the den, nor even when he slipped and nearly breached her scalp again. He plodded onward through the brush and did not breathe a word—his frenzied captive's feral pleas were all that could be heard.

They found themselves beside a bog that bordered on the cave, and Ful tried to forget the hope he could no longer save. He pulled the crone up by the crown till she was on her knees, then spoke the subtle words of vengeance softly to the trees.

He did not look back as he left, still silent and alone, and was not near enough to hear his monstrous mother moan. The willows would make certain that she suffered for her crime, imprisoned deep in waking sleep until the end of time.

His rancor spent and quest complete, the Ghost
then realized that what he'd sought was surely not
as he had fantasized: a life of retribution had led
headlong to the worst, for wrath gives nary nour-
ishment and scorn can slake no thirst.

A thousand years untethered did the demigod
endure, but all the world was drained of drive
and held no more allure. Ful asked wherefore he
should remain but could not answer why, and so
he broke his earthly yoke and rose into the sky.

He shuttles now among the stars and scans the
lives of men, in hopes of finding grounds enough
for living once again. His spectral sheen can oft be
seen above us as it burns; it is our lot to wait and
watch for when the Gray returns."

The song was sung. Whispers raced around the storyfire,
growing louder with each step of the Teller's withdrawal from
the roundhouse. Timmet, however, was not there to hear.
Moving about nimbly in the blind cool of his family's hut, he
continued his preparations for the journey ahead.

He snuck to the rear wall of the hut and carefully arranged his trapper's chain on Ruya's sleeping mat—he knew
his younger sister had always coveted the thing, and he suspected she would need something to soften the blow of his
sudden departure. The young hunter slid back to the center
of the space, chanting words he couldn't remember learning
as he hung a string of freshly dressed rabbits above his grand-
mother's greatchair. Back at his own mat, he slipped a few
salted rations and a bundle of gierleaf into his pack before
lashing it between his shoulder blades and then moved to

retrieve his spear from its hiding place in the rafters. Lingering at the doorway only long enough to make sure he wouldn't be seen, he stole out of the hut into the evening air.

The timberline fell away and the terrain turned rockier as he climbed out of the crescent valley that cradled the village. From the top of the ridge, he could see the entirety of his homeland, fixed in shades of silver. Closing his eyes, he saw it by the light of day: a rolling blanket of jade, cut through with a vein of meandering blue. It was a beautiful place, and he loved it, but he knew it had become too small. The expanse that greeted him from the far side of the ridge, however, was fresh and frightening, and he inhaled its wonder deeply.

He sucked on a sliver of the leaf he had brought with him as he tested the earth underfoot and relished the rarefied air. Myriad stars glinted against the black; even diminished in the humbling presence of the moon, they were beyond counting. There was one which shone more brightly than all the others: a smear of light which sped steadily eastward before disappearing beyond the horizon. Timmet fixed his eyes on the point where the star had met the edge of the world and marked his new destination.

His mind returned to his kinfolk for a time as he negotiated his slippery descent into the unknown. He pictured their faces, as he had so often seen them, gazing in awe as the Teller wove her harmonies; he wondered if her voice would ever again flood his mind with waking dreams. He had a feeling the answer was unknowable, and that the matter would soon be out of his hands.

Perhaps one day, though, she would sing his song.

Nemesis

The infiltrator appeared as a binary shift in their midst. Light whorled and shone in his Dreadknight armor, transforming his diminutive form into a quasar. Even in the near-vacuum of space, they could sense the sphere of pulsing, crackling energy expanding around him. His intentions were clear.

For a moment, stillness reigned: there is no fear among dragons, but sometimes there is prudence.

Bilrog was the first to break the trance and sing the hymn of blood—she was the most intemperate of their number, and her comrades had yet to succeed in cooling her ready rage. Her jaws snapped and gnashed; her tail coiled and whipped in an iridescent frenzy of bladed scales and lithe muscle. The interloper was unmoved by the display—even as the whirling mass of death drew nearer, his only perceptible movement was a slight tilt of the head. A smirk, perhaps? Simple curiosity? Bilrog had overcommitted, and she would not live long enough to find out. The knight rolled under the sweep of her tail, boosting as soon as he was clear; Bilrog's neck rippled outward from the point of impact, shattered against the battering ram of the killer's knee. A second movement rent her jaws asunder, and the tear of her maw was sent racing down the length of her powerful form. Spasming halves of the she-dragon drifted off into space; the globules of black blood left hovering in their wake spattered the knight's armor and stained the faces of Bilrog's kin, who, with anger in their hearts, set upon the assassin with all their might.

The Dance of a Thousand Deaths had begun.

||||||||||||||||||||||||||||||||||||||||||||||||||

Syrtok appeared, as ordered, in the Hall of the Fiercest. With carnage still fresh in his mind, he felt more uncomfortable than ever to be in such a place, which had not seen violence since its onimium slabs were first cut from the quarry. High above him, five elder dragons gazed down from their gargantuan roosts. They lowered their heads in unison to inspect the drakeling warrior, their slow, misty eyes seeming to peer through him; he saw his form reflected in the metallic sheen of their teeth, and it was clear that the battle had diminished him. As was customary, he deferred to the ancient ones, waiting for them to address him before he spoke.

"Blood and Ash unto you, Son Syrtok," the Fiercest said in chorus. "We were pleased to receive word that our Rul-Shikk warriors repelled another incursion by the Shameful Ones. What have you to report?"

"Venerated Fiercest," he began, searching for a way to sweeten his words, "it is an honor to know that you are pleased by our deeds, but I hesitate to deem the mission a success. We lost dozens of our brethren to the assassin before he finally fell beneath the weight of our onslaught. I fear we must enact a new strategy if we are to withstand the growing threat posed by the Unscaled."

"That will be for us to decide," the Fiercest echoed. "Tell us the reasons for the change you desire, young one."

"Our ranks are dwindling. Even our strongest females are no match for the Dreadknights," Syrtok said, nearly pleading. "If we lose many more, the brooding rate may not recover." The dragon commander lowered his gaze from the cragged faces surrounding him. "Bilrog was among the fallen. Her brood has not yet received word of her fate."

"We are aware of Daughter Bilrog's martyrdom, and she will be honored in the highest order," the Fiercest respond-ed together. "A glorious death in battle would have been her wish."

"It would have been her wish to come home to her brood!" Syrtok cut across, the flint in his teeth emitting a shower of sparks as his jaws crashed together. He tried to cover the loss of composure, but the damage was done—he saw the faces of the Fiercest harden, the mist in their eyes illuminated by the primordial fire within.

"Where do you imagine yourself to be, whelp?" they boomed, ringing the hall and Syrtok's ears.

"Forgiveness, my Fiercest," Syrtok said, genuflecting. "I am still under combat's duress—it will not happen again."

"See that it does not," the Fiercest answered, their ire re-treating. "As for the matter at hand—we have already given orders which implement the change of which you speak. It is the word of this council that you and your slayers are to remain planetside to protect the brood. Our presence will be bolstered at each of the slip points. Seven additional Cytis-class hulks per point should be sufficient to repel any further attacks."

"Seven hulks?" Syrtok snapped, his civility nearly forgotten once more. "If our elite are no match for the Dreadknights, what good will lumbering artillery do? One of their assassins can kill scores of our Rul-Shikk. What if the enemy decides to send even two? What if they send a proper army?"

"This council possesses no evidence that the Unscaled have the capacity of which you speak. All attacks have thus far been carried out by a single agent. Movement through the slipstream requires enormous energy expenditure—it is unlikely that our enemy can send multiple entities simultaneously." Syrtok opened his mouth to protest, but the Fiercest preempted him. "Our decision stands."

Syrtok stared into eyes that had grown too cloudy to see the truth; he searched them for a sign of salvation, but saw only death staring back. He did not intend to accept his quietly. Bowing deeply, he bade his elders farewell. "I hear and obey. Blood and Ash, my Fiercest."

"Blood and Ash, Son Syrtok."

Syrtok turned the words of the Fiercest over in his mind as he loped along the path back to the hall's gates. Riljj awaited him just outside.

"What was their judgment?" the young admiral asked eagerly. "Are we to have our war?"

"Their decision was as feeble as their minds," Syrtok answered. "We are to increase our fortifications and deploy more Hulks to the slip points."

"Hulks? They'll be useless against the Dreadknights. They're far too sl–"

"I have already expressed that sentiment," Syrtok replied before his protégé could finish. "They would not be swayed. We do not—and will not—have their consent."

"Then we are doomed!" cried Riljj.

"It is true that our current course leads nowhere but our end—we have no other choice but to proceed unsanctioned. We must launch our offensive on the invaders' homeworld at once."

"Into their nest? On our own?" Riljj asked. "How can so few hope to prevail where the enemy is strongest?"

"We do not know that their strength lies at home. Indeed, I suspect the opposite," Syrtok said. "Their attacks come with increasing frequency—the pattern implies urgency. Urgency can easily turn to desperation."

"What reason could so powerful a race have to despair?"

"You are too young to have seen a giant go dark, Brother," Syrtok said, motioning to the heavens. "When a sun reaches its end, it rages and flares and throws all manner of fire and violence out into the unknown. I fear we are dealing with a dying star."

Riljj grew silent for a time. "You have never led us astray, Brother Syrtok," he said at last. "You know that we will follow you into the arms of death, should you so command. What would you have me do?"

"Gather the remaining Rul-Shikk," Syrtok instructed. "All but Thraxx—his loyalties lie with the Fiercest. Rally at the mouth of the Keltus Belt slip point and await my arrival. There is a matter here which requires my attention before we embark."

"It shall be done," Riljj said with bow. "Blood and Ash, Brother Syrtok."

"Blood and Ash," Syrtok replied solemnly.

As Riljj took flight and sped in the direction of the unassuming rookery the Rul-Shikk called home, Syrtok reached to retrieve an object from beneath his wing; the blackened heart beat faintly within its crystal encasement, the last remnant of the most ferocious warrior Syrtok had ever known.

Clasping the offering of commiseration in his foreclaws, Syrtok began his long walk to the Hovelgrounds with all the haste that decorum would allow. Bilrog's brood was owed its due, after all, but war was not known to wait.

Slack

Gilbert was breaking in his new armchair and trying to lose himself in the business section of the paper when Dennis hovered into the room, dressed in the same clothes Gilbert had seen him in the day before. Dennis flopped into the empty spot on the couch across from his roommate and didn't rebound; the cushions started to consume him as soon as denim touched suede.

"Morning, sunshine," Gilbert said. It was three in the afternoon on a Sunday.

"Morning," Dennis mumbled.

"Everything good?" Gilbert asked. There was no great cause for alarm just yet, but Dennis had a way of deteriorating rather suddenly.

"Just spinning my wheels is all," Dennis replied. "I can't seem to get anything to stick."

"Your uncle was a good man," Gilbert said sympathetically, "and I know my compass would be a little off if I had all that inheritance dropped on me."

"I keep telling myself the money shouldn't change anything, but it just does," Dennis said. "I feel like a cheetah at the zoo."

"Have you tried getting out of your wheelhouse? Maybe you just need a new perspective."

"Yeah, I tried my hand at painting, but nothing doing. Look," Dennis said, shunting a thumb over his shoulder at a small canvas that Gilbert hadn't noticed hanging by the hall door. It depicted a woman on a horse, poorly. "I gave writing a shot, too, but all I could manage was a pretty thin volume of bad poetry. I don't even think you could call it a book."

"Hmm. What about writing lyrics?" Gilbert asked. "Bad poetry makes for good music. Popular music," he corrected himself. "Everyone makes fun of bad poetry all the time, but I'd bet most of those people listen to some kind of pop..." he trailed off as his gaze wandered up into the corner over Dennis's left shoulder. "Hey, Den," he squinted, "how long has that stain been up there?"

"Since the beginning of June, I think," Dennis said without looking up from the furniture catalog he'd found. "Pretty sure it stopped growing in August."

~~~~~~~~

Gilbert closed the front door with his heel and squatted to set down a stack of binders on the dining table; he shrugged a bag onto the nearest chair.

"How was the protest?" Dennis asked through a mouthful of breakfast. He was carrying a substantial amount of cereal around in the front of his shirt like a fruit picker.

"*Demonstration*. 'Protest' is a loaded word," Gilbert said with a wince. "Went well. There was a counter-demonstration, but we outnumbered them about four to one. Crazy that some people are still so resistant to progress. What's going on with you?"

"Going a little crazy myself, to be honest," Dennis said, reaching into his cereal pouch with his free hand. "I think I need to just go somewhere and express my glands. Like, out in the woods on my own, get creative for a couple weeks."

"Glands?" Gilbert asked, unadorned bafflement in his voice. "What glands?"

"You know, like a dog has scent glands in its butt that have to get expressed, otherwise the excretions get all backed up and rank and the dog is completely miserable. You're supposed to do it on a regular basis—keeps the stuff from getting so foul and saves you a lot of anguish. Sometimes you have to help the dog."

"I'm a little afraid to ask how you help the dog," Gilbert said.

"You stick a finger in its butthole and squeeze the stuff out of the gland manually. That's what I used to feel like whenever I was stuck in the apartment or at work all the time and didn't have any time to work on my own stuff, but now it's like that all the time. My creativity glands get all backed up and then everything I do is pedestrian shit and I have to get someone or something to help me along. The someone or something usually isn't very good for me, and I can't say that I haven't wound up with an actual finger up my ass before. I need to find a way to express my glands before it gets to that point."

Gilbert studied his friend's face as if it were one of those find-the-difference puzzles.

"Den, I don't want you to take this the wrong way," he said, "but you're the weirdest person I know."

"Fuck," Dennis stomped. "I just remembered I have to renew my license next week. Why the hell do they make it expire on your birthday? Shittiest present ever."

"You should probably focus. And not do what I think you're about to," Gilbert said from his seat at the kitchen table, nodding at the saucepan in Dennis's hand. "Use a funnel."

"It'd just be one more dish to clean. I got it," Dennis said as he removed his homemade pizza sauce from the stovetop and prepared to pour it into the mason jar waiting on the counter; he bit his bottom lip and closed one eye to line everything up. The failure was unmitigated, splattering sauce all over the floor and speckling both men's pants with a rich, clingy red.

"Well," Dennis said, looking less sheepish than Gilbert thought he should have, "can't blame me for being an optimist."

"True," Gilbert conceded. "Sometimes optimism and stupidity are the same thing, though."

～～～～～～～

Gilbert returned from a jog, surprised to find his roomie with his nose in the newspaper.

"Anything good in there?" Gilbert panted as he removed a suite of sweatbands.

"You never think about how many people die every day," Dennis said, still engrossed in the paper.

"I try not to dwell on it," Gilbert said. "Obituaries?"

"Monty Stellhalter, Viggo Miller, Janet Peabody. Here's one—listen to this: Richard E. Vittorio, beloved husband, grandfather and friend, died peacefully on the morning of Monday, October 13, 2014. Mr. Vittorio was ninety-nine years old. Following a memorial service on Wednesday, Richard was committed to his final resting place at Hillcrest Cemetery. A native of Camden, New Jersey, Richard was born March 2, 1915 to Alfonso and Julietta Vittorio. Richard was a decorated Marine marksman who served his country in the Pacific Theater of the Second World War. His hobbies in later life included travel, numismatics, and restoring his many cars, all of them 1959 Chevrolet Impalas. He is survived by his three children and seven grandchildren." Dennis looked up when he was done. "Can you believe that? What a waste."

"Sounds like he lived a long, full life," Gilbert shrugged. "What's the problem?"

"He lived to ninety-nine years old. He couldn't have held out another year to clear a hundo?" Dennis looked at the paper again. "Not even a year—five months. Way to quit, Dick."

"You're definitely not writing my eulogy," Gilbert said, kicking off his running shoes.

"I wonder how many people they find after the fact, like, how many people sit there for a while before anyone catches it," Dennis said, letting the paper fall open onto his lap. "It has to be a lot, right? I mean, I haven't seen anyone die, personally. I don't think most people I know have, either. A bunch of people die in the hospital, but it's definitely not all of them."

"Can't be," Gilbert agreed. "The first one you read, Monty Stellhalter. What does the obituary say?"

"Not much," Dennis said, scanning the page. "Name, birth and death dates, sorely missed by family and friends." Dennis turned the paper to Gilbert to demonstrate that he wasn't over-simplifying.

"He jumped off the roof over at Shiller, Mendelsohn and Ross last week," Gilbert said solemnly. "Twentieth floor."

"Jesus. Did you know him?"

"No, Tina told me about it," Gilbert answered. "She said the firm brought in a trauma counselor on retainer.

Apparently there was no warning that anything was wrong with the guy."

"Suicide is fascinating. I can't imagine ever doing it myself," Dennis said airily. "I wonder what the guy's last thought was."

"I think every suicidal person probably thinks the same thing just before the lights go out," Gilbert said.

"What's that?" Dennis asked.

"*This is a mistake.*"

~~~~~~~~~~~~~~~~~

"Check out the *conejo* I picked up for dinner," Dennis said as he waggled a skinless length of muscle and teeth at a traffic-weary Gilbert. "Butcher had them on sale."

"Yikes," said Gilbert, loosening his tie. "What's the occasion? You never miss Chinese night."

"Getting out of my wheelhouse, like you said," Dennis replied, rifling through the knife drawer. "The more I thought about it, the more I realized I wasn't really pushing myself enough."

"Good for you," Gilbert said, freeing himself of his silk noose. "So, what's on the menu?"

"Well, this little guy is getting roasted," Dennis said, patting the carcass on the rump, "and I'm going to sauté up some mushrooms and shallots to go with. I had to go all the way down to the coast road to track down shiitakes. You know, that place with the green awning?"

"Weird," Gilbert said in a far-off tone. "I dreamt about that place last night."

"Yeah?" Dennis asked as he pinned the naked rodent to the cutting board with his left hand. He took aim with the cleaver in his right.

"I was chasing a leaf blowing down the sidewalk, but it kept getting away from me," Gilbert said. His eyes traced a crooked path on the floor. "Do you think that means anything?"

"Probably," Dennis grunted, his hand streaking earthward to relieve the rabbit of its head.

~~~~~~~~~~

Dennis was covered in cereal dust and being swallowed by the couch when Gilbert wandered into the living room. He was still wearing his work clothes, even though his weekend had started several hours prior.

"Everything good?" Dennis asked, propping himself up on one elbow to get a better look at his friend. Gilbert was wearing an expression that Dennis had never seen on him before.

"Not really," Gilbert said, falling into a heap next to Dennis and staring off at nothing. "That was my dad. They think my mom has Alzheimer's."

"Oh, shit," Dennis said, struggling to adopt a more distinguished posture. "I'm sorry, man."

"I should have done more to prepare myself for this," Gilbert said, his expression still vacant. "You think about your parents falling apart when they get old, but it's all so abstract until it actually starts happening."

"I'm going to be a mess when my folks go," Dennis said absently; he joined Gilbert in staring. "Probably won't be much longer now, unfortunately. Dementia runs in the family. Both sides. Vicious fucking thing."

The room filled with a long silence, but it was not an uncomfortable one. Dennis was the first to speak again.

"I dig these conversations we have, Gilbert."

"So do I," Gilbert said, sinking further into the crease between the cushions and trying not to think too hard about the stain in the corner. "I think they keep me grounded."

Message

Mary is holding her husband's phone, because he forgot it at home again. She found it on the table in the foyer when she called to tell him to pick up a gallon of milk. She doesn't know what to say when the police call to say they found her husband at the bottom of the embankment.

She comes down to the morgue like they ask and identifies the body, which is his. They say his car was parked by the side of the road, and the flashers had run the battery down to almost nothing. She starts to ask why they mentioned that, but then figures it out on her own. They tell her they found him on his back with his dick out. They don't use those words, but it doesn't really matter.

They also say they found a handheld dictaphone near his body, but that the water in the ditch ruined the thing; they can't even get it to turn on. She says it likely doesn't matter, because he kept it password-protected. They say they probably could've overridden that, but then repeat that it's a moot point, because of the water. They ask if she thinks it odd that he had it with him under the circumstances. She tells them that he couldn't leave work at the office, and that he took the little recorder thing with him everywhere. She doesn't tell them that she threatened to book a flight home when he tried to give dictation on their first Jamaican getaway, and that he called her bluff. She did get him to agree to limit it to an hour a day. He fudged the numbers, but he took her dancing.

She asks the police where all of his things are, like his clothes and his wedding ring, because he's naked under that sheet and the things have to be somewhere. They tell her that her husband's effects are back at the station in lock-up. She asks when she can have the things back. They say they don't suspect any foul play, but that it's policy to hold potential evidence for two weeks before it gets remitted to the next of kin. Mary says she'll busy herself in the meantime.

Two weeks later, she gets off the bus and walks the block and a half to the police station.

There isn't much to collect. His ring, a plain but heavy gold band with thousands of little scratches in its surface, comes out of the manila envelope first. She puts it on her middle finger, but it slips off again. It fits on her thumb, so it stays there. She tries not to think about the fact that she buried him without it. Watch and wallet, both gifts from her, appear next. The watch is caught on the little flap of the wallet that holds extra credit cards, but they get the two untangled before she sets them to the side. A bottle of cholesterol medication follows; she tells them they can throw it away, but they inform her she needs to take everything with her. She says she'll throw it away in the dumpster in the parking lot. They tell her it counts as hazardous material, and that she'll have to dispose of it properly. She says she will, but really she'll throw it in the dumpster. Next, the dictaphone clatters onto the counter. She asks about it, and they say they were never able to get it working. She looks at the condensation on the inside of the display and flicks the power switch a few times before she places it next to the watch. Last out of the envelope is his key ring. Mary recognizes all of the keys but one. She asks about his clothes, which aren't there. They say thanks for reminding them, and they come right back with the bag. She asks them what's wrong with the clothes. They tell her that his clothes got all soiled from the mud and torn up from the brambles and trying to resuscitate him. She says it's okay, because she always hated that suit on him, anyway, and tells them to just chuck the bag. They reiterate the rule about taking everything. She acknowledges, and doesn't mention that she will throw the suit in the dumpster. They offer to put the things back in the envelope for her; she declines and scoops everything into her purse with her forearm. They tell her how to get to impound from there, so she can pick up the car. She says thanks before she leaves.

She walks over to impound and finds two attendants in the office trailer; she hands some papers to the more motivated-looking of the two. He says they'll waive the storage fee on the car, seeing as Mary is bereaved and all. It takes him almost fifteen minutes to bring the car, because someone moved it from its original spot and didn't enter it in the logs and he had to tow it over from the far end of the lot. The bottom of the car is caked with mud, and there is gravel jammed in the treads of both tires on the right-hand side. She'll stop at a drive-thru car wash on the way home. She thanks them and pulls the keys out of her purse; she tries to start the car, but the battery is dead, because of the flashers. The more motivated-looking attendant returns with a battery pirated from another car and some jumper cables. Mary pulls away after another thank you.

The next day, she drives to an electronics repair shop. There's a buzzing noise coming from the passenger side of the car, probably because the car wash didn't get the gravel out of the tires. The buzz turns into a hum when she drives faster, so she drives faster.

The youngish man at the shop inspects the recorder that Mary hands him. He says he's never worked on one of these, but he can look up how to do it real quick. Mary examines a couple of machines with green displays and lots of knobs while he's in the back room. He comes back and says he found some information about that particular model. She asks if he can get the recording off of there. He says something she doesn't understand about the accessibility of flash memory. She asks if that means he can get the recording off of there. He says he might be able to, but that he can't guarantee the work. She says she'd like him to try.

Later, he calls her over to a computer behind the counter. He says he was able to get to the files, and that he can transfer them to a memory stick if she has one. She says she doesn't have one, and asks if he can put it on a CD. He says he doesn't have any CDs, but that he can send the files to her in an email. She says she doesn't know how to do that, and asks if she can just listen to the files here. He says she's welcome to, but asks if she doesn't want to have the files at home. She says she does, but doesn't want to wait to listen to them. He says it's no skin off his back and shows her how to open the files before he returns to his workbench to finish the repair job he was doing when she first came in.

Mary dons the headphones sitting next to the keyboard and proceeds as the man showed her; he can see her over the top of the monitor from where he's sitting, but the flux vapor rising from the circuit board he's soldering stings his nose and makes Mary look a little blurry. She clicks on one file after another and squints every few seconds. He tries not to look at her, because it's probably something personal that she's listening to. She clicks through some more files until she stops clicking and lets one of them play all the way through. She covers her face, and tears fall through the spaces between her fingers and run down the backs of her hands as her husband, dying in a ditch by the roadside, speaks the last words he'll ever say to her.

The man at the workbench wipes his averted eyes with a shirtsleeve and tells himself it's on account of the solder.

Polyamory

When I leave her, when I come home to my family, there's a kind of shift that happens. It's a resistance to the movement, as though I'm walking through hip-high water or leaning into a strong, steady headwind. It could be the weight of my conscience, but I'm not sure I've ever really had one. I know what the word means, but I'm pretty sure understanding isn't enough—I think you're supposed to feel it. Do you have a conscience if you've never felt guilt? Maybe it's possible for certain people to change, but I don't count myself among them. I don't know that I would change, even if I could—there's not much impetus to do things differently if you reject the concept of regret.

Listen. I love my wife. I love our children, and I love our dog and our cat. Hell, I even love my in-laws, most of the time. Problem is, I also love my girl. Why should those things be mutually exclusive? Why should I feel guilty, and why should the others feel betrayed? From my point of view, I'm doing nothing more than sharing all the love I have to give and spreading joy to as many people as possible. If anyone should feel guilty, it's those cynics who would condemn me for trying to make the world a happier place.

It's just after sundown when we find ourselves here again, the two of us. I don't remember much of the drive over. The family thinks I'm at a trade show in Duluth for the week.

After we're done, she rolls over and asks if it bothers me that I'm so much older than she is.

I tell her that I think being old is really a matter of giving up. There are plenty of people who live to an advanced age but never get old. They're just lively and warm, and they pack it in one day when their heart decides it's done beating. The others wind up with gnarled knuckles gripping plastic handles. For those ones, it starts with that first recoil, that time you thought better of it. You feel a little too sore after a workout one day, so maybe not so hard next time. Don't want to hurt yourself, do you? Move a little less here, think a little less there. After a while, you stop learning new things, stop doing new things, stop growing. You spend all day inside the same four walls and wake up at the same time every morning and go to bed at nine on the dot and play cards with the same boring people every Friday. You don't know why you do it anymore, but you don't really think about it too much, either. Then one day, you do think about it, and you realize you haven't had an answer in twenty years and that you've become too rigid to change course. Then you die, not because you have to, but because you can't see any reason not to.

She tells me I'm depressing her and asks if I want to fuck again.

It's a more athletic session than the first—not that I have anything to prove—and she's still writhing under the sheets when she whispers the ultimatum, barely louder than breathing: *Leave her.* Setting aside my feelings about the timing, I have to admit it's a strong tactical move. I probably should have known better than to think it would never come.

I pull her to me and look deeply into her eyes. There is love there, without a doubt. Whether it is greater or less than the other is anyone's guess.

Dealing

The ramshackle man sitting across from Kay raised an eyebrow as his eyes followed the stack of bills through the air; the cash made a satisfying thump as it landed on her desk. The man looked from the money to Kay and back again.

"Correct me if I'm wrong, Mrs. English," he said, "but that looks like quite a bit more than the fee I quoted you. You sure you don't want to count it again?" Jon Greening had come a long way in the world of private investigation, and experience told that gifts were grounds for suspicion. He waited for his client to illuminate him.

"I didn't take you for someone who'd negotiate against himself," Kay said, leaning back into the plush embrace of her executive's chair. Greening's expression didn't change. "I thought you might appreciate a bonus for a job well done," she finally capitulated. "And I'd certainly appreciate your discretion about the things you've been looking into for me. You never know—I might have another job for you one of these days if it turns out you know how to keep things to yourself."

The P.I. had leaned forward to pick up the bundle of bills and was flipping through, a noticeable rise creeping into the narrowed corners of his eyes and mouth as Kay spoke. "Consider my lips sealed, boss," he said. "Here's to our future—may it be long and fruitful." He saluted her with the wad of cash before stowing it in his interior coat pocket.

Kay made a move to stand, but Greening insisted that he show himself out. "I won't think any less of you, Mrs. English," he said. "Cross my heart." Holding his right hand out over the desk, Jon the Digger took his leave with a *been a pleasure*.

When the man had driven out of sight, Kay rose from her seat and crossed the room to an imposing rosewood built-in. A gentle push on a burnished brass handle revealed a battalion of bottles in a mirrored compartment. She grabbed a snifter from a nearby serving tray, turning the glass upright as she pulled the stopper from a whisky decanter sporting a golden chain; the space filled with the smell of someone using a well-made dress shoe to grind out an embargoed cigar. She poured herself two fingers and thought things over.

Perhaps she had been too absent, or Roy had. Whichever it was, at some point or another she'd realized she no longer trusted the man she loved. The nagging feeling had started small, but her suspicions had quickly become too insistent to ignore. She'd contacted Greening through a mutual client, who had extolled the investigator's trustworthiness and attention to detail. The rest had all moved too quickly to remember.

Walking laps around the office and fidgeting with her glass, Kay kept her eyes on the wainscoting instead of the elephant in the room: the snoop's gift was still lying there on her desk, sealed with a wide band of packing tape. As she paced, she thought about everything that was already in place in her life. Mostly, she thought about success. She had a successful business. She had successful children. Even her marriage was successful, by most measures. Shaking any one of those pillars would risk toppling the whole arrangement. There was certainly the option of just destroying the envelope and forgetting what had really only been conjecture up until that point, but that didn't address the issue of her dignity. Was it worth sacrificing that to save the rest? Thirty years earlier, the choice would have been easy. Now, she wasn't so sure.

Hiring Greening might well have been enough of a response. She and Roy both had the truth, in different forms—it would be a simple matter of opening the envelope if she ever wanted the question answered with unadulterated honesty. As things stood, she felt she could forgive Roy whatever he might have done, but to see hard evidence confirming her fears would take things past the point of reconciliation. She knew herself, and she knew she'd never let him live it down.

She stopped at the framed family portrait on the wall opposite her desk: she and Roy, the boys and Dhalia, summer at the lake house, happy and whole forever. She wished they could take another picture like that. She also wished the kids would call more often, but she'd come to terms with the fact that life runs its course. She tipped her glass and downed the rest of the scotch.

The floor safe chirped as it popped open, its heavy door held ajar by sprung hinges. She had set the code well before her misgivings had taken identifiable form, and she knew Roy could get in if he wanted to—he'd yet to forget their anniversary. She would have been justified in re-coding the lock given the circumstances, but sentimentality can be tenacious.

She reached into the safe to remove her mother's jewelry and the stack of deeds sitting at the bottom, laying the unopened envelope in their place and taking particular care with her fingers as she closed the safe door again; the locking code summoned a resolute clank from the box. She replaced the hardwood panel that hid the safe's location and then drew herself up from the floor, straightening her suit jacket and brushing the dust and ache from her knees.

She thought of the ride home and what she'd say to Roy when she got there. Portrait smile at the ready, she was hopeful something would occur to her on the way.

A Funny Friend

Sandra wrenches the cork out of a bottle of red wine as she tries to remember the last time she was this angry at Kevin. She hasn't been, she concludes. This is a superlative moment.

Over the years, she's gotten used to Kevin's sense of humor oscillating between hopelessly unfunny knock-knock jokes and jarringly tone-deaf pranks; she's even had a genuine giggle every now and then. Unfortunately, things are on the prank end of the spectrum this time, and it's gone too far.

It started innocently enough three days ago: Sandra snatched up her buzzing cellphone, connected the call, and yelled from arm's length at the person on the other end of the line. "Hold on, I'm working," she said. "Let me find my headset." After a bit of paper shuffling and a few peeks under the desk, she remembered that she had left the missing earbuds at the office. "Sorry, Kev," she said, the phone by then clamped between the side of her head and her shoulder. "Just trying to finish up some stuff from that one project." The reports she'd been working on were overdue, left unfinished by one of her lazier coworkers. Sandra had a feeling Caroline wouldn't be around much longer.

"On a Sunday, San? That's lame," Kevin squawked, his voice smothered in the hair above Sandra's right ear. "I guess I won't keep you, then. Just wanted to say 'bye' before I head off tomorrow morning. I'll be out of radio contact while I'm gone."

"Shit," Sandra said, slapping her palm to her forehead. "I forgot you were going out of town. I wanted to grab lunch before you left."

"We can do it when I get back," Kevin offered. "How's Thursday look for you?"

Sandra corralled her planner from the edge of the desk and flipped through a few calendar pages. "It's a date," she said, switching the phone to her left ear and scribbling the words "Lunch" and "Kev" into Thursday's box.

"Can't wait," Kevin replied. "Hey, before I go: *Knock, knock.*"

"Who's there?" Sandra asked, not missing a beat.

"Otto."

"Otto who?"

"Otto know, who are you?" Kevin answered.

"You're an idiot," Sandra said with a laugh.

"No argument there," he replied. "Okay, I should probably run. I haven't even started packing."

"Shocking," Sandra deadpanned. "Have a good trip, big guy."

The two said their farewells, and Sandra spent the rest of the night engaged in a caffeine-fueled marathon of report writing.

"Fucking Caroline," Sandra thought as she stood in the shower the next morning, trying to will herself into wakefulness. She really should have been able to sleep in on her first day of vacation, but now she was going to have to sit in rush-hour traffic to get those reports in. She pegged the faucet

handle into the end of the blue zone and felt her pulse race as her skin constricted, fingertips and nipples throbbing. The shock helped sharpen the edges a bit; Sandra was glad that she wouldn't have to guzzle down any more coffee. When she was lucid enough and relatively clean, she contorted herself out of the tub, stuffed her clothes into the hamper and made her way to the bedroom. She'd kept her hair dry so that getting ready wouldn't take so long; she made herself workplace-presentable and headed for the garage.

It had been the sheerest optimism to think that she'd be able to get in and out of the office unmolested. She managed to avoid getting roped into any actual work, but finagling her way out of there had taken nearly as long as it would've to just do the damn things they'd asked of her. She arrived home a few minutes shy of noon; she kicked off her flats as soon as she was inside, hung her blazer on the coat rack by the front door, and dumped her purse on the dining table. After rummaging around in the refrigerator for a while, she plopped down in her favorite spot on the couch with a bowl of yogurt. She was just beginning to enjoy the situation when her purse started ringing.

She'd already sprung from the couch when she realized she could have just let it ring: she was on vacation, after all, and there was no one she could imagine wanting to talk to right then. Her irritation grew upon seeing an unfamiliar number on her caller ID; she declined the call and was about to head back to the couch when the phone rang again. She picked up.

"Hello?" Sandra said; it sounded more like a demand than a greeting.

"Hey, you," a strained voice answered.

"Who is this?" she asked, still accusatory. She was unconvinced that she knew anyone with such a gravel-timbered voice.

"Oh, come on. One guess."

With her patience nearly exhausted after the freak show at the office, Sandra reckoned she could hazard exactly one guess. "Kevin, is that you?"

"We have a winner."

"Ugh. I was about to start screaming," Sandra said, loosening her grip on the phone. "I thought you were supposed to be incommunicado while you're at the conference."

"Yeah, the conference. I didn't go. I think I must have caught that virus that's been going around. Opened me up at both ends—I don't think I slept at all last night."

"Aww, you poor thing," Sandra cooed as she returned to the couch and her bowl of yogurt. "No wonder you sound so bad."

"Thanks. That's exactly what I need right now."

"Sorry, that came out wrong. I just meant your voice sounds different," she said, a guilty twinge knotting her stomach. "Weren't you supposed to be giving a presentation at this thing?"

"Yeah. I got someone to cover for me," he said. "They'll have to make it work."

"That's too bad. I know how hard you worked on that."

"I'm over it. I can't really focus on much apart from the nausea right now, anyway."

"I can imagine," Sandra said. "Hey, what's this number that showed up when you called? I don't recognize it."

"Oh, that. My phone fell in the toilet last night during one of my evacuation sessions. Fun stuff."

"Shit."

"No, it was just puke that time."

"Hilarious," Sandra jabbed. "So, new phone?"

"New old phone. It's just a burner I picked up in case I

travel somewhere a nice one would get lost or stolen. Lot of good that plan did, huh?"

"Well, at least you can get a hold of people," she said. "Hey, you want me to come over, bring you some soup or something? I dropped those reports off this morning, so I'm officially a free woman for the next two weeks."

"I bet your friends at work are going to miss you," he said. "You probably shouldn't come over, though—you don't want to catch this thing. I don't really think I'm ready to put anything in my system just yet, anyway."

"Are you sure?"

"Yeah, forget about it. I'm doing well enough crawling around on my own."

"If you say so," Sandra said. "But make sure you drink plenty of water, Kev. You're probably pretty dehydrated by now."

"I'm way ahead of you."

"Oh, yeah?"

"I'm so far ahead, I'm coming up behind you."

Sandra chuckled a little at this and took the opportunity to sign off. "Okay, big guy. I'll talk to you tomorrow?"

"You know it. I'll drop a line when I'm up and about."

Sandra spent Monday's remainder catching up on all the crossword puzzles and TV shows she'd been missing on account of work. She also treated herself to the box of Girl Scout cookies she'd squirreled away. It was sublime.

Tuesday's call found Sandra sunbathing on the patio at midday.

"Hey, Kev," she said after retrieving her phone from its place on the little garden table next to her chaise.

"Hey, you."

"Everything okay?" she asked.

"Yeah, no cause for alarm," he said. "I just missed your voice."

"Oh," Sandra said, not knowing what else to say. She and Kevin were best friends, but it was not their modus operandi to share their feelings so openly. She chalked it up to his compromised condition and tried to move on. "How are you feeling?"

"Still pretty crappy, but I seem to have stopped gushing, so I guess that's an improvement. What are you up to?"

"Not much. Went shopping earlier. Just lounging on the patio and enjoying doing nothing right now," Sandra said blissfully, turning to worship the sun. "You forget how nice it is not having anyone making demands on your time. I may never go back to work."

"Somehow I don't believe it."

"I know. I have an addiction," she said, not entirely joking. "The first step is admitting it, right?"

"You got it." There was a pregnant pause followed by a short intake of breath. "So, what are you wearing?"

"That's kind of a weird question," Sandra said after she was sure she hadn't misheard him. She was wearing some grody old shorts and a ratty t-shirt she'd had since high school. It was hardly sexy attire, but the question still made her squeamish. "Why would you ask me that?"

"Sorry, I'm just trying to picture you while we talk. It feels like forever since I saw you."

"Huh," Sandra huffed, shifting a little in her seat while she mulled over whether to give him the benefit of the doubt. "I'm back in my pajamas," she said after convincing herself the question was probably innocuous. "Not planning on going out again today."

"Nice. Did you shave your legs this morning?"

The question made her stomach jump, not least because she had, in fact, shaved that morning. "Hey, I think I have to go," she said through the frog lodged in her throat. "I don't know—it could just be your flu talking, but you're kind of creeping me out today. I'll talk to you later."

She realized she had hung up without letting him say goodbye, but she wasn't in the mood to call him back right then; the conversation had made her feel the same way she did whenever she thought there might be a spider crawling on her. The sensation remained even after she had folded up her lounge chair and cleared her things from the patio, so she resolved to go for a jog. Running usually helped clear her mind, and she hadn't worked out since before the weekend.

The exercise did the trick. Sandra returned home drenched in sweat and freed from the creeps the phone call had engendered, which had been replaced by the fresh conviction that she should finally make that attempt at writing a children's book. Several hours, a lackluster dinner and two vodka martinis later, she was sleeping upright on the couch, surrounded by wads of crumpled paper. The notepad on her lap was empty except for the underlined heading *Benny Bunny Buttons* and the sentence *Benny Bunny Buttons liked to bake bread.* The hall light bifurcated the living room with a skinny slice of incandescence; the television beamed into the room with no one to listen, a pulsing countdown timer and phone number superimposed over the crotch of a plastic-smiled man selling garbage to people with weak impulse control.

Sandra spent her Wednesday morning indulging in a breakfast that was clearly too generous for any one person. Once she had finished her third mimosa and finally gotten up the gumption to clear away the leftovers, she set her mind to getting a little work done. She could only enjoy idleness in infrequent doses, and the recent days of lazing had already pushed her to the limit on that front. She'd also been putting off doing a serious cleaning of the house for months. It was time.

She was thoroughly disheveled and more than a little grimy by the time she finally reached the bathroom. It was her least favorite room to clean, which probably explained why it was the one that needed it most desperately. As much as she loathed using hardcore cleaning products, everything in the bathroom was so caked with soap scum and mineral deposits that the vinegar solution she'd been using on the rest of the house simply wasn't going to cut it. The armistice was off; she swallowed her pride and prepared for chemical warfare.

Three-quarters of an eye-watering hour later, she rinsed everything down one last time and opened the window to let the room air out. She waited until she was back in the hall with the bathroom door closed before removing the bandana covering her mouth and nose, which had become a necessary accessory any time she was forced to use the caustic, store-bought stuff.

She was still gathering her supplies when she heard a loud knock at the front door, followed by several rings of the doorbell. Of course, the bathroom was about the farthest thing from the front door; she stubbed her pinky toe on the coffee table as she speedwalked by and was still cursing under her breath when she finally got to the entryway. The cursing became louder and more explicit when she opened the door to find nothing but a view of impending twilight. Goddamn teenagers.

Her curmudgeoning session was cut short by a vibration in her pocket. She checked the screen and picked up only after admitting to herself that she really needed someone to talk to right then; her sick friend's gravelly voice greeted her from the other end of the line.

"Hey, you," he said. "How's your day been?"

"Well, it started out great," Sandra said, heading into the kitchen and trying to forget their previous conversation. "But it's been on a pretty steep decline since I started cleaning this morning. I spent the last hour inhaling toxic fumes, and I just got ding-dong-ditched and nailed my toe on the coffee table." She hiked her foot up onto the counter. "I think I might actually lose the nail, now that I'm looking at it. I could kill those little bastards—I was going to get a pedicure later this week, too."

"Sounds pretty rough."

"Why are you whispering like that?" she asked, suddenly aware that she was straining to hear him. "Don't tell me you're losing your voice."

"Seems that way. I feel pretty good otherwise, though."

"Kev, you've got to take better care of yourself," she said. "I think we should probably call off our lunch date tomorrow, don't you?"

"Sure, we can push that," he said. "I'm sure we'll see each other soon enough. I have a surprise for you."

"You know I hate surprises," Sandra said. "What is it?"

"If I told you, it wouldn't be a surprise."

"Can you give me a hint?" she asked.

"I guess I could do that," he rasped. "I can tell you this—you should probably shave your pussy ahead of time."

The reflex sends her phone skittering away; it comes to rest just short of the counter's edge. She's fixed to the spot, staring at the little black rectangle and fighting to keep her chest from heaving at what she just heard come out of it. Beside herself, she grabs a glass and a bottle of wine. Her eyes water a little as she tries to wrestle the cork out of the neck.

The poisonous words replay on a loop in her mind; when she eventually gets the bottle open, the distraction has thrown her aim off. She topples her glass mid-pour and sends a wave of wine rippling across the counter. Guttural aggravation escapes her as she grabs a fistful of paper towels and tries to sop up the mess before it soaks into the butcher block.

With the emergency clean-up over, she calls Kevin back to give him a piece of her mind; several attempts to the new number yield nothing but incessant ringing. Thinking he might still have access to his voicemail account, she dials his old number and tries in vain to swallow a lump when the ringing stops.

"Hi, you've reached Kevin McClellan," her friend says in a healthy and uncharacteristically professional voice. "I'm unable to answer your call right now, but if you leave your name and number, I'll get back to you as soon as I can."

After the beep, Sandra gurgles into a tirade. "Kevin, I just wanted to tell you that I don't appreciate the way you've been treating me. You know I've been under a lot of stress at work, and I don't need you messing up the only chance I have to relax. I'm sorry you're not feeling well, but that's no excuse for you to do this to me. Don't call me again unless it's to be supportive." She hangs up, applying pressure to the END button as if the binary slave in her hand could somehow convey the sentiment behind the gesture.

The phone rattles and shimmies on the counter a few minutes later; she leaves it where it is and continues pouring herself a new glass of wine. He can leave a message if he wants to, but she's going to let him dangle for a while. Halfway into her glass of wine, however, the temptation of the blinking voicemail icon on her phone hasn't subsided. Her resolve wanes just long enough for curiosity to get the better of her.

"Sandra, it's Kevin," her friend says in a rare tone of distress. "Listen, I don't know what you were talking about in that voicemail you left. I've been at the conference since the last time we talked, and I definitely haven't called you. I haven't called anyone—I've been slammed the whole time I've been here. I'm not sure what's going on, but I promise it's not me. Shit—my phone's about to die on me. Look, I'm still at the convention center, and my charger is back at the hotel, but I can tr–"

Sandra replays the message several times, but it always cuts off at the same point. Repeat listening doesn't change the unsettling gist, either.

Her mind ties itself in knots trying to reconstruct the conversations of the last few days. Of course she's been talking to Kevin. Of course she has. Didn't he say it was him when he first called, when he said he'd gotten sick and missed his business trip? He must have. She can't remember if he did. In fact, she can't remember the person on the phone having said anything that only Kevin would know. His voice had been different, but she had just chalked that up to his being sick. She spins her wheels trying to make the puzzle fit together until a piece finally clicks into place: she was the one who had first said "Kevin". He had made her guess.

That cold shower feeling returns, and the spiders are everywhere. A tremble breaks out in her hand so suddenly and violently that she drops her wineglass, which detonates against the tile floor. She fumbles with the phone; her ragged breathing plays polyrhythm to the beat of the unanswered ringback. In desperation, she leaves another message for the Kevin she knows is real. "Kev, I really hope you're not fucking with me right now, because I'm freaking out. If you are, I'll try not to be mad, but you have to stop. Please, please call me back as soon as you get this."

She hangs up and tries to figure out how to live with the silence; she wishes there were someone else she could call. "I don't think I can handle this right now," she admits to the empty room, her fingers trailblazing in her hair as her palms come to rest on her temples. She grabs the open bottle from the counter and leaves everything else as it is. Cabernet runs confused routes away from the glass starburst on the floor, saturating narrow seams of thirst grout as it goes.

She enters the bathroom to find it once again full of breathable air; a stark absence of glass shards all over the place also makes it a distinctly more comfortable place to be at the moment. Setting the wine bottle down on the vanity, she shuts the door behind her and hurries over to the window; the sash meets the sill, halting the cold draft pouring in from outside. She latches the window and yanks the still-fluttering curtains across the span; the feeling of privacy is welcome. She returns to the vanity and takes a swig straight from the bottle, moving the wine around in her mouth and waiting for it to strip some of the tension out of her shoulders. She reaches over to plug in the radio perched on top of the toilet tank; the tinny speakers scream to life, blaring static and ramping her already debilitating anxiety. She scrambles to find a station, ultimately landing on classical and adjusting the volume to a comfortable level. She winces and breathes deeply through her nose. When she opens her eyes, she stares at herself in the mirror and forces a few more deep breaths. Another pull from the bottle nudges things back out of the red.

She leans over the tub and turns the faucet on full blast; a roar of scalding water echoes in the empty tub as she moves to prepare the rest of the space. She squats at the vanity and coaxes a few half-melted candles out of the jumble of disused toiletries packed into the floor cabinet. The matches take a while longer to find; she almost relents and goes back to the kitchen for a lighter, but they turn up underneath a stack of shower caps pilfered from a motel she only vaguely remembers having visited. With the lights dimmed and candles flickering through the steam filling the room, she lets her clothes fall in a little pile at her feet and dips a toe into the bathwater.

She braces on either side of the antique clawfoot and lowers herself slowly, stopping just before a certain sensitive region touches the steaming surface. Clenched buttocks make several tiny retreats before she inhales sharply and drops herself in, gooseflesh breaking out everywhere and all the fine little hairs on her thighs pulling bubbles down into the water. Her pain threshold sneaks up on her; she wonders if she's made the water too hot, but the urge to escape soon subsides. She settles in, a cool enamel edge cradling the nape of her neck as droplets of sweat swell at her hairline.

She hasn't washed her hair in days; it's been nice to have a little extra sheen, but now the unctuous feeling on her scalp and the back of her neck is nearly unbearable. She lifts her feet from their braced position on the floor of the tub and pulls her knees to her chest, plugging her nose with her upper lip and squeezing her eyes shut as she slides below the surface. She hangs in a liquid chamber, and the world outside the tub is blunted. Her senses refocus her own internal functions, magnified: pulse thumping, stomach growling, joints creaking. Her perception turns further inward, and it dawns on her just how long it's been since she's been alone with her thoughts. It's a shame, she thinks, but possibly for the best. It's only when she's composed and collected that her mind doesn't try to betray her at every turn, and collected is the farthest from what she's been lately: there's the constant chaos at the office, her click-clacking biological clock paired with a conspicuous lack of a significant other, the general guilt and insecurities of womanhood, and now this bullshit on the phone.

She tries a meditation technique she's been reading about: she lets her negative thoughts come, lets the chaos roll into her consciousness, and then attempts to do nothing more than acknowledge the thoughts and let them continue on their way. At first, it feels like she's being swallowed whole, like the usual anxiety is going to crush her in a vise, but then she does as the method dictates, repeating a mantra in her head while she hums an intonation. The bubbles streaming from her nostrils carry her troubles away as the tub reverberates all around her, and the stranglehold begins to loosen. Her worries lose their moorings and drift off, slowly at first, but then carried away more and more quickly in the current. They are replaced by nothing at all, and for a few blissfully bewildering moments, she is completely at peace. The serenity is fleeting, though, as it suddenly occurs to her that she urgently needs to surface for air. She plants her feet again, shifts her center of gravity rearward and emerges from the water.

She has just enough time, through streaming water and sticking eyelashes, to make out the shadow looming over the tub. A pale hand reaches down from the darkness to meet her, and she feels its latex grip, firm and exacting, tighten around her throat.

In a flash, she's underwater again. At first, all Sandra can do is stare dumbly through the stinging foam at the menacing silhouette above her. Then the thrashing begins. She claws and kicks, trying to pull herself out of the water, but the tub's freshly-scoured enamel is too slick; her joints ricochet off its surface, dull thumping on a buried bass drum. At one point, a sharp snap reaches her ears as her weakened pinky toe breaks against the inside of the tub, but the pain signal is overridden; she doesn't need that little piggy to survive. She thrashes even harder.

She feels the grip on her throat loosen slightly, but the hand refuses to let her surface. Water rushes down her now-unconstricted airway and into her lungs—the feeling flips a further switch in her lizard brain that adds coughing to the bucking and thrashing. With her face still situated entirely underwater, the violent tussive fit fails to do anything but fill her lungs more completely with sudsy panic. She feels the stinging deluge slosh around inside her as she struggles, the weight of the water pinning her to the floor of the tub and pressing her tender lungs into the gaps at the back of her ribcage.

Her quaking hands flail above the surface of the water, searching for any opportunity for purchase; they find nothing but the arm of the shadow, so that is what they take. Fingernails puncture and rake, lacerating stoic flesh. Droplets of blood jet and swirl as they enter the water, fogging Sandra's fading vision even further. The shadow is unmoved.

Sandra knows that the end is coming. An unwelcome sense of calm is accompanied by an oceanic hiss, and all at once the fight goes out of her arms and legs. Though her brain is busy trying to kickstart her vital organs, she is vaguely aware of the fingertips that have come to rest on her carotid artery, sitting there softly enough that they rise and fall with each desperate beat of her heart. Time elongates as her vision collapses to a single point of twilight. Just as she is about to give herself over to the inevitable, the hand wrenches her up out of the water once more.

The urgency of life rushes back in, restoring Sandra to semi-consciousness and a senseless clash of form and color. The uncontrollable coughing resumes, and an impossible amount of soapy water is expelled from her chest cavity, punctuated by a mouthful of wine-colored bile. The urge to scream, greater than any she's ever felt, is left unfulfilled; her spastic lungs can't pull in enough air to produce anything more than a hiccuping whimper. Her arms are ropes at her sides, and there's nothing to be done when she feels a second rubberized hand cup the back of her head. Thin lips pull forward over a toothy grin to grace her forehead with a single, delicate kiss.

She's under again, but the immediacy is gone. It's clear now that there's no reason to fight anymore, if there ever was one. She can also see that this moment is no worse than any other in the thirty-two years that preceded it. She remembers one that was worse, actually—the one when she first realized that her grandpa wasn't happy anymore. She holds on to the memory as her heart slows to a stop at the bottom of the tub.

She sits on the edge of the vanity, making the occasional blind attempt to pick up the wine bottle at her hip. The bottle doesn't cooperate. She's doing her best to stay focused on the action in the tub, but she feels like she's viewing the entire ordeal through the wrong end of a telescope: the edges are crisp enough for her to understand the thrust of what's happening, but everything is so flat and jittery that she can't make out the details. She's jolted from her concentrated state by a whisper in her ear.

"Knock, knock," says a familiar voice.

"This isn't a great time," she says, trying to refocus.

"Knock, knock," the voice repeats.

"Seriously, Kev."

"Knock, knock," the voice insists.

"*Fine*. Who's there?"

"Dwayne," says the voice.

"Dwayne who?"

"Dwayne the bathtub, I'm dwowning."

"Damn it, Kevin," she says, her eyes fixed on the motionless figure being dragged from the water. "That's the funniest thing I've ever heard."

Wet Work

The rumblings about a government recruitment effort were proven true when a matte green flatbed arrived at the shipyard. Men in fatigues wielded bullhorns to draw a crowd and make their case. When they had finished, hands were raised in the crowd—some eagerly, some with trepidation—and their owners were loaded onto the truck. Zhang took his place among them.

Zhang had long thought that his talents as a welder were squandered on work as menial as repairing ships that had fallen victim to shallow seabeds, incompetent captains or old age, and he hoped the soldiers had something more challenging in store for him. Though he dare not express his enthusiasm openly, he had always preferred undoing the damage dealt to ships intentionally by environmentalist saboteurs or clandestine international skirmishes. He loved to see the way that torpedoes from deniable navies or the hurtful gifts of dreadlocked frogmen could render flat, cold steel into something fluid and beautiful: razor-edged flowers bloomed for him just under the waterline, and the tough skin of alien beasts—peeled away by the hands of an absent giant—sizzled at the tip of his asklepian torch. As the truck pulled away from the harbor, he wondered which sort of work this new endeavor would be nearer.

He surveyed the faces of the men and women jostling in the bed of the truck with him, but no discernable pattern volunteered itself. There were two other welders, several longshoremen, a crane operator, and a handful of others who, as far as Zhang knew, were merely the docks' resident mahjongg players. The motley crew of recruits sat unspeaking as the truck trundled along the dirt road, with most of them gazing off into the countryside or staring at the scuff marks on the boots of the man watching over them. They were a dozen or so miles outside the city limits when the man with the scuffs produced a box full of hoods and ear plugs, which he distributed without a word to Zhang and the other newly-concerned passengers. When two of the tilestackers asked why their senses were being confiscated, the man responded by hammering on the roof of the cab with his fist and telling the driver to pull over. The skeptics were left stammering in a roadside dust cloud.

The hood was itchy, but Zhang found he could suppress his urge to scratch by closing his eyes and focusing on the crystalline darkness that formed in the center of his vision. He peered into the coalescing black until the faces of his family emerged. His wife and daughter smiled lovingly back at him from the abyss; his daughter waved a pudgy hand from her hoisted position in his wife's arms. He hoped he would be able to send them a letter soon.

He lost himself in the reunion until the crystal cracked some hours later amidst the smell of diesel fumes and his realization that the truck was no longer moving. An unseen hand grasped the peak of his hood and not a little of his hair, and all gentility was spared as he was undraped into a flood of artificial light and nudged to his feet with a lacquered rifle stock.

He tried to take in what he was seeing, but the sudden luminosity after hours of darkness severely limited his ability to parse the information. The only things he could immediately understand were that he was one among many in this open-air compound and that each of the visitors there seemed to be in some stage or another of training. His comprehension scarcely improved as he marched with the others along rows of concrete pylons to a bunker where, after supplying his personal and next-of-kin information on the form the clerk shoved at him, he was summarily laden with the trappings of his new life.

The following days were marked by uncertainty for Zhang and the other inmates of the camp. They were forbidden from speaking to anyone but their overseers, and even then could only speak when spoken to. The bunks assigned to the workers were individually compartmentalized and soundproofed, and each bed could be entered or exited only via an externally lockable, rectangular panel running along its length. At the end of each shift, the workers would bathe, shuffle into the mess hall to consume their rations of rice and pickled fish, and wait for the colorless barracks to narrow and hush as the guards sealed them away for the night.

When they weren't locked up in bed, the men and women spent their time following orders and executing tasks at various stations inside the compound's high walls. A great many of the attendees were clearly out of their depths, their graceless hands and restless eyes belying their earlier pronouncements of competence in their respective professions. Zhang's group was led to a row of dangling, knotted ropes, which they were encouraged to climb without the use of their legs; to their right was a large diving tank in which candidates were apparently demonstrating their longevity in the absence of breathing apparatuses. On a large tarp next to this tank, a number of people were being instructed in the use of scuba gear. This was a skill which Zhang already possessed, and he wondered if he would have to prove as much.

The cycle of toil and hibernation made the days pass with dizzying speed, with each sundown marked by a thinning of the herd. The day's rejects were told to return the items they'd been issued upon their arrival, and they were given no meal before being loaded into the back of a truck. It was never announced just where the trucks were headed when they left, and the remaining workers were too kowtowed to dare ask, though many hypotheses ran silent through their minds. None of the imagined possibilities were pleasant.

By the fourth week of their stay, the workers' ranks had dwindled to fourteen. The group was roused early one morning and harshly encouraged to leave the barracks, whereupon they were compelled to board an idling truck which awaited them in the courtyard. The vehicle differed from the one which had delivered them to the compound only in that it bore a camouflage canopy skinned over a lattice of thin metal rods. Zhang saw his own disquietude at the abrupt end to their tenure mirrored in the faces of the others; the hoods and earplugs were back, though, and the modicum of nostalgia helped in its small way to calm the passengers' nerves.

The farewell journey from the camp was hard to distinguish from that of the arrival. Zhang's family dissolved at the same point in their fractal visit, again in an acrid haze of unspent hydrocarbons. Hair-pulling, bewildering light and rifle stocks rounded out the resemblance.

The seafront where the workers were made to disembark from the truck was as foreign a place as any to Zhang. The sky was obscured by a borderless wall of clouds whose pallor seemed to drain the color from the world below it, and the seaside itself was featureless save for a long concrete pier. The uniformed men's boots squeached against its spray-dampened surface as they escorted the group to a large factory trawler moored at the end of the dock. Based on the rusted joints in its hull, Zhang could tell that the fishing vessel had seen several decades of hard service and very little upkeep. The marines who awaited the workers aboard the ship looked somehow even less amiable than the soldiers returning to their vehicles; their motionless faces were so wind-polished and deeply-hewn that they more resembled statues than men.

The trawler launched without fanfare, accompanied solely by the sound its propellers made as they chided the ship away from the shore. The wan clouds overhead loosed a curtain of rain that blotted the coast from Zhang's view before he could form a lasting memory of the moment. Speakers bolted to the boat's superstructure crackled to life to announce that the bunks below deck were to be filled by nine o'clock and that lights were to be out by ten. It seemed a reasonable arrangement compared to the forcible seclusion of the training camp barracks, and the fourteen exhausted passengers did not protest.

The following morning, serial blasts from the ship's air horn drove the workers from their cramped accommodations and up to the messdeck, where they were instructed to collect their morning meals from the galley; breakfast consisted of the same pickled fish and rice they had been given ashore, with the addition of three segments of pink citrus per worker. After the meal, the workers were ordered topside, where Zhang watched a pair of marines lower the flag at the stern of the ship and replace it with one he did not recognize.

A number of hand signals were made available to the captive crew: these were explained via illustrated cards distributed by the marines. Right hand up meant that vomiting was incipient. Left hand up meant that the lavatory needed to be used in one of the two conventional ways. Zhang counted himself lucky that he hadn't yet experienced the impetus to raise his right hand; he was in rare company. The distinction between right and left hands wound up only being useful at the very beginning, as the head was subsequently befouled so severely and often that the marines deemed it off-limits to anyone but them. The disbarment meant that the workers could regularly be seen hanging their posteriors off the side of the ship and relieving themselves into the windy void above the waves.

There were a number of other terms in the new sign language, as well. Right hand covering nose indicated that a fellow crewmate had been seen breaking one of the ship's many rules. Left hand on right shoulder communicated that someone had been injured. Both hands up meant that another ship had been spotted. When this signal was used by any one person, all others who saw the signal were required to make it, as well, in order to ensure that the sighting met with minimal delay on its way to the marines' attention. As this information was circled in red on the card, Zhang made a priority of committing its particulars to memory.

Five days after the mainland had disappeared, the boat was pushing through empty seas as still and smooth as polished marble. By this time, the captive crew knew to keep their eyes off of the uniformed ones, who acted quite aggressively whenever they felt they were being scrutinized.

Some of the workers had begun to grow restless, but as they were forbidden from talking to anyone about anything at all, they merely gave each other meaningful looks, examined the flaking enamel on the railings of the ship, and traced the pilgrimage routes of the many six-legged stowaways aboard the ship. The mahjongg players had taken up their mantles once more—thanks to the unexpected providence of the marines—and Zhang found it interesting to watch the unvoiced gesticulations that ensued whenever a player was suspected of cheating.

Two nights later, Zhang awoke to the sound of men shouting to one another and the ratcheting clangor of the ship's anchor being winched into the sea. A bass clank accompanied the end of the anchor's chain, and Zhang felt the trawler's massive engines sputter and die. His grogginess, along with the fact that the berth was still completely dark, told him that dawn was likely hours away. He tried to remain awake for as long as he could in case the marines were planning on explaining the bedlam, but after some twenty minutes, he was forced to give himself back over to his weariness.

After breakfast, the workers were ordered to line up at arm's length along the perimeter of the ship. Zhang found a place near the prow just in time to see a marine with a stack of envelopes come into view. Walking from one worker to the next, the marine examined the number embroidered on each person's lapel, riffled through the stack, and produced the packet with the matching number stamped across it. It was announced that the contents of each envelope were for its owner's eyes only, and it was made explicit that the prohibition on sharing applied equally to fellow crewmates and marines.

After all of the envelopes had been distributed, the marines informed the laborers that they would have one hour to study the plans before starting construction. This seemed painfully short to Zhang, but he was unprepared to be the first among them to voice an objection. He opened his envelope to discover a set of blueprints for what looked like a large sphere, along with a construction-oriented addendum to the hand signal chart they had received previously. Upon closer examination of the blueprints, he established that the sphere was meant to be very large, indeed: the scale printed on the sheet indicated that the structure would be several times larger than the ship they were on. Duly intrigued, he found a quiet corner of the ship where he could pore over the diagrams.

The scale and scope of the work to be done was mind-boggling, and the undertaking would have been difficult enough on dry land. Even so, the underwater construction progressed at a blistering pace in the weeks thereafter. The laborers found the huge, curved steel ingots which would make up the sphere's outer hull hovering below the waves, held aloft by thick shackles that ran up to buoys at the surface; the crane aboard the ship had shed its trawl net in favor of a specialized cable attachment which could handle the ingots' titanic weight.

The laborers worked in pairs, and despite the fact that most of them had never even talked to one another, they were able to collaborate well enough by using the provided hand signals and following the directions issued by the marine foremen over the communicators in their diving helmets. Zhang's assigned partner was charged with wrangling the thick bundle of cables that powered his welding electrode; it was an arrangement which freed Zhang to set up the hyperbaric conditions necessary for the job and bring his skills to bear unhindered. As there was no way for him to find out his partner's name, Zhang simply assigned him one. He imagined the name "Duo" was as likely as any.

Zhang and Duo would usually sit together during meals and the infrequent breaks in their work, and though they would sometimes try to converse with the aid of their eyes and minute gestures, it wasn't the primary focus of the meetings. Most of the time, the simple proximity of a friend was enough.

After one such sit-down, Duo excused himself to go below deck. Zhang felt a twinge as his companion left, but he was also glad to have some private time, such as it was. True privacy was all but impossible on the ship, so Zhang used the chance to spend some time with his own thoughts. He reached into the hip pocket of his coveralls and retrieved a small laminated photograph of his wife and daughter he had taken several years earlier. His portable family had survived hundreds of dives with no ill effects apart from a slight clouding of its protective plastic jacket.

Early one morning, the workers were shaken from their beds by a storm of biblical proportions. Zhang hoped that the marines would call for a work stoppage on account of the fact that there was less than a full day's work required to finish the project, but his hopes unraveled when they announced that construction would proceed as planned. Through sheets of lashing rain, the marines asserted that the terrified workers would be much more comfortable underwater than on deck, anyway.

The marines' claim was only partly true: while the storm's rancor was clearly more frightening above water, the workers still had to contend with everything below the surface—including the nearly-completed sphere—shifting by several forceful meters with each surge. The conditions had them scrambling, but somehow they managed to make several hours of stuttering progress in the gaps between the waves. Then, just as it felt like the storm was beginning to wane, a momentous swell careened through the construction zone, rocking the ship to such an extreme angle that the tip of the crane nearly kissed the water. The lifting cable went slack for a moment, and when it found its tension again, the downward momentum of the large steel segment it had been carrying was translated into a brutal underwater arc. One of the female riveters had swum into the unfortunate position directly between the humongous, pendulating sphere and the crane's runaway payload. She didn't stand a chance. The force of the impact left her corpse crushed into a freshly-gashed divot in the sphere's thick plating; the others were forced to look on in stymied panic as their comrade's broken body twitched out the last of its will to live.

Once the storm had passed, the workers heard the series of tones over their earpieces that signified the order to return. Back aboard the ship, a marine ordered one of the laborers to explain what had happened. After removing her left hand from her right shoulder and being chastised for her stupidity, the woman gave her most faithful recounting of the accident. As soon as she had finished, one of the uniformed enforcers disappeared below deck, reappearing a few minutes later carrying a full set of diving gear. He donned the equipment without a word and then joined one of his compatriots in a pontoon dinghy suspended at the trawler's starboard side. The diver sat on the edge of the small boat as it was lowered into the water, rolling backward into the sea shortly after they touched down; his head resurfaced a moment later, and he trod water long enough for his fellow statue to pass him a weight belt that one of the more buoyant workers had previously been using. The diver was not gone long. When he returned, he did not have the drowned woman's remains with him. The belt was gone, as well.

Just before nightfall on the next day, with the final welds and rivets in place and the ship's deck awash with floodlight, the workers stood at attention along the perimeter of the ship once more. Each laborer was given a small bottle of plum wine and two hours to relax and celebrate the project's completion. However, few of the men and women were in a celebratory mood, and most drank their wine in passionless gulps while avoiding contact with the others. Zhang observed a few of them slipping the bottles into their pockets, but he could not think of a compelling reason to follow suit.

Waking the following morning, Zhang found it odd that the ship's engines were still silent. He also realized that he had not yet heard the anchor being hoisted and wondered what the cause of the delay might be. Their work was done, and he could see no ready reason they should need to linger.

Having left their neatly made beds, the workers reported once more to the galley, where they were greeted not by the mess cook, but rather by the dourest of the marines, who ordered them to report above deck prior to receiving their morning meals.

Topside, the mood did not improve. After a protracted silence, the speakers screeched on, and the voice of the captain rang out over the whitecaps. With a theretofore absent warmth to his voice, he lauded the workers for their performance and encouraged them to be proud of their work, assuring them in the same breath that their country certainly would be. What they had done, he said, would secure the nation's place in the pantheon of world power for generations. He also said that before they could return to the mainland, the workers would need to be searched in order to make sure that nothing of crucial importance to national security had made its way into any of their pockets. He politely requested that they line up, turn to face the sea, and clasp their hands behind their heads.

Exchanging surreptitious glances, the workers moved to do as they had been told. As they took up their assigned positions along the ship's bulwark and prepared themselves to be frisked, they could hear the remaining marines descend from the pilothouse to join the ones already on the deck. The soldiers fanned out and stood at attention, one behind each laborer. None of them made a move to search the waiting captives.

Zhang had turned to face the sea like the others, but he did not raise his hands. As he looked out over the water at the unbroken horizon and the empty sky above it, some part of him remarked the sound of precision-machined metal parts sliding into place directly behind his head. He was also vaguely aware of the clamor that broke out shortly thereafter, but even that was soon indistinguishable from the sound of waves surging against the hull of the ship. His hand found its way into his hip pocket, where he ran his thumb gently back and forth around a smooth, laminated corner. Preparing himself for one last dive, he breathed deeply and filled his lungs with cold, salty air until all that was left was the sting.

Ounce of Prevention

I live in the dark. It hasn't always been this way. I used to know what my world looked like.

Back then, father showed me how everything worked. He had to, he said, in case something happened to him. I always hated it when he said that, and I always told him so. Discretion, he said, was the better part of valor. I think he was probably right—father was rarely wrong. He died six months ago.

Time does not pass quickly underground. It was forever ago that father shook me out of bed and into the waking world, pressed my bug-out bag into my hands (*always be ready to go, and go for good*), and ushered me out onto the back porch and down the steps to the backyard. The dew on the lawn made the places between my toes cold and slippery and it soaked heavy rings around the bottoms of my pajama legs. They swung back and forth like bells, slapping and sticking against my ankles. It bothered me until I remembered the dry change of clothes and pair of sturdy shoes in the canvas sack clutched to my chest. The thought was warm. I asked where mother was, having noticed she wasn't with us. She'd be fine, father said, and hurried me along.

The car was not parked in the garage as it usually was—we had to walk down the block and around the corner to reach it. Father told me to stay out of the bright circles the streetlamps made on the sidewalk. I tried to make a game out of it, but father didn't want to play. We could play later, once we got there, he told me. We would have nothing but time.

The first days were the hardest. I had to use the toilet in front of father, which I hadn't done in years, not since he used to help me do it. The metal cylinder in the corner was cold and too high off the ground. The backs of my legs always had imprints from the rim when I was done. Father did not help me.

We played chess and read books. I had courses in chemistry, botany, philosophy and survival tactics, and I did my daily aerobic exercises so that I wouldn't atrophy and stunt. Father lamented that he couldn't give me better food to eat, being that I was a growing girl. MREs and canned fruits were all that we could count on down here, though, so that was what we had. Things had to last a long, long time if we were going to make it through.

The banging started a week after we climbed down. Father said the doomed people outside were trying to get to us, and that we absolutely could not let them in. He told me we'd almost certainly die if we did, but assured me that the hatch at the top of the ladder was hidden and secure. It wound up not mattering—it sounded like the doomed people got close at one point, but then the banging receded and didn't return. Father put the rifle back on its rack without unloading it.

He still keeps me company, in his own way. It's not the same as when he was really here, but I appreciate that he's trying. I've just had to come to terms with the fact that some things are different, and that they're not going to go back to the way they were. Father's face is never going to have that weight to it again, and I'm never going to feel the scratch of his two-day whisker kiss on my cheek. Life soldiers on, just as he said it would.

Father told me that if the lights ever went out, it would be for one of two reasons and that in either case, we'd need to start the other clock. When it got to zero, it would be safe to go outside again. I used to be scared that things would go dark, but I'm not anymore. At least now I know how much longer I have to be down here.

Apart from father, I miss my books the most. I know all the stories, and I can recite them all from memory, but I miss seeing the words on paper.

Remembering just isn't the same.

═══════════════════

The man in the black uniform with shiny black holster and shiny brass buttons keeps shaking his head and looking down at his feet. She knows he is talking to her; she can see his lips moving. There is no sound, though, and no meaning to the movements of his mouth. He finally makes eye contact and tips his hat as he turns to leave.

The world crashes back into her ears, and her hand snags the officer's right sleeve from behind. "Ma'am?" he says as he turns to face her again.

"Say that again, the last part. The last part, say it again, please." She hasn't loosened her grip on the man's sleeve.

The officer pries her hand gently away and holds it with both of his own. "I said there's nothing more we can do at the moment, ma'am. I'm sorry, but we have to call off the search. If you come across any new information, you let us know and it will go into the case file. We'll let you know about any developments on our end."

She follows the man outside and watches him walk down the long concrete pathway leading back to the street. She watches him get into his patrol car and softly close the door. She watches the patrol car become a black-and-white blotch at the end of the street. Then she is alone.

The piece of paper clutched in her left hand has grown soft from folding and unfolding, and the oil left by her fingertips lets the light pass through the fibers. She need not have kept the note; its message, scratched out in a hectic hand, will never leave her memory. She smooths the page on the porch railing and looks once more at the words gouged in blue ink:

Taking Melissa somewhere safe. You will not find us.

Kissin' Boots

The two older boys flashed broad grins at the one supine in the grass, but the cruelty in their eyes belied the show of civility. This was bad news for me, seeing as I was the one staring at the sky.

"He is but low, wouldn't you say, Gerard?" the bigger of the two said, shaking his head as he leered down at me. I had been upright just a moment earlier, but the boys had rectified the situation.

"He is indeed, Hagar, he is indeed," chortled the other, nodding. "I wonder though, d'ya think he's worthy of rine-shining my trompers?"

"Very-zery, Gerry," Hagar answered emphatically. "Just look at those quivering lippos he's got. I bet he's hiding a stupendous lapper in there."

"Hags, I do believe you're on to something," Gerard responded, index finger on chin.

"That's a luck, too," Hagar added. "One would need a gigantish, zoonging tongue to get your steep ones clean. And look—you've gone and stepped in a pile, haven't you? Double luck!"

Our heads all swiveled to examine Gerard's generously-heeled boots, which were indeed plastered in a rather dark and malodorous semisolid. I crawled up onto all-fours and put on what I hoped was a defiant face—I had no intention of giving my assailants the gratification of knowing I was scared very nearly out of my wits. It was at this point that I regretted not staying on the path through the park. Better yet, I could have given the park a miss altogether. Lesson learned.

"What kinna shite are you two building over 'ere?" boomed a voice from behind the trolls. The man who had just emerged from the other side of the hedge which hid us from the footpath sported a burning red mustache which jumped out against the grays and browns of late autumn, and his neatly shaven head was slick with the drizzle that had started. He was taller and wider than either of my new friends, and he absolutely dwarfed me.

"Get out of 'ere," the man rumbled without looking down at me. "I'm to 'ave to 'ave a speak with these youngs."

He didn't have to tell me twice.

The potential taste of boot leather and mystery excrement was still fresh in my mind as I stumbled from tree to tree in the woods that abutted the park. The soft, uneven terrain made it all but impossible to concentrate on anything but staying upright, and when I finally realized how silly I must have looked and how little progress I was making, I stopped to lean against the nearest tree and scanned my surroundings for some kind of landmark. Based on how long I'd already been underway and the direction in which I thought I'd likely been traveling, I should have been somewhere in the vicinity of Winthrope Way by then. Not least on account of the glaring absence of well-groomed rows of pretty little cottages, I suspected that something had gone awry. After a healthy round of deliberation, however, it seemed premature to re-trace my steps so soon. I collected myself as best I could and pressed deeper into the woods.

The drizzling rain drew to a close as I walked, and the light passing through the loosening clouds and empty tree branches cast a crawling tapestry of dim shadows across the forest floor. The earth underfoot had a damp, vegetal smell that reminded me of Nana's cellar and the treasures I used to find down there as a child. I indulged myself in the reverie for some time, and while the nostalgic interlude was pleasant enough, it wasn't long before I once again began to worry that I wasn't making enough headway on my homeward journey.

Just as I was reconsidering a backtrack, I was startled to a halt by a sudden, loud buzzing. At first, I thought I might have inadvertently trespassed and tripped an alarm of some sort. I jumped back to unbreach whatever line I may have crossed, but the buzzing didn't cease. The noise seemed to be directional, and by swinging my head from side to side, I determined that the sound was most intense when I looked into the thicket to my left. I had no desire to spend the night in the wilderness, and as the buzzing was all I had in terms of a lead out of my predicament, I gave in to my impulses and ventured toward the source of the sound.

After several hundred contorted paces through the thick-et, I entered the clearing whence the buzzing seemed to come, where I was dutifully shocked to see—rising into the air some hundred feet above me—a step pyramid consisting of large, irregularly masoned stones. The structure's lack of symmetry was such that it was really only nominally a pyra-mid, but I'm sure no one but an architectural stickler would have challenged the designation. Had I been asked my sur-mise, I would have said that the monument had been built in several non-contemporaneous stages, based on the various materials used and the wildly inconsistent quality of construction. I had seen similar patchwork masonry on some of the structures that had been repaired in the thin years after the Great War, but even the newest portion of the pyramid looked to be at least several hundred years old.

I circumnavigated the pyramid and took in all there was to see. Rudimentary wooden ramps shot zigzag patterns up each of its four faces, with each ramp starting at a different height and ending higher up in an open archway mortared into the side of the edifice. None of the ramps appeared to reach the very pinnacle of the pyramid, which was adorned with a curiously out-of-place gazebo, painted brilliant blue. At ground level, there were three deep, parallel trenches which extended from the base of the pyramid on one side; steps led down into these channels, each of which terminated beneath the base of the structure in an opening spanned by scaly iron bars which did not readily divulge whether they were meant to keep something in or out. I could not see very far into the dark beyond the bars, but I could hear the faint rushing of water somewhere in the distance. My pen light was of little assistance in the matter, insofar as it succeeded in doing nothing apart from startling a family of rats on the other side of the barrier.

As soon as the novelty of my discovery had worn off, I returned to the matter of finding a way home. I tried to establish the cardinal directions by referring to the position of the sun, but the resurgent cloud cover and incessant buzzing made concentrating on the process quite difficult; I also realized that the information would be of little utility given the fact that I didn't know where the devil I was. In a flash of inspiration, I thought I might be able to use the gazebo's elevated vantage point to regain my bearings. If nothing else, getting inside had the potential to muffle the buzzing a bit. I made my way to the bottommost of the pyramid's wooden paths and began my ascent.

After climbing roughly a fifth of the way up the structure and overcoming my fear of the dark, I entered the portal at the top of the ramp. My pen light did a satisfactory job of lighting my way, and with the buzzing sound fading a bit more with each step, I followed the torch's bright oval through the labyrinthian passages that awaited me within the pyramid. I had made heady progress and a score of turns when, much to my chagrin, my light began to fade rather rapidly. I broke into a run, but my haste was of no avail; somewhere in the middle of the maze, the torch went out.

Without the aid of my light, I figured that the best way forward was to keep one hand on the wall at all times; it might not have been the most efficient way of moving through the imbroglio, but it did ensure that I wouldn't lose any ground. I had continued on in this manner for at least as many turns as were behind me when I saw a hint of indirect light glowing from around the next corner. I breathed a sigh of relief as I rushed toward the sunlit exit to my ordeal.

My relief promptly dissipated when I found that I was on the side of the pyramid opposite the one I'd entered, but hadn't gained any appreciable elevation. It also struck me that there was no way down from my current position—other than a jump that I was nowhere near optimistic enough to attempt—and that no matter which way I re-entered the pyramid, I was going to have to brave the blind maze at least one more time. As I had already come so far and still needed to establish where I was, I elected to continue the climb and attempt the maze at the top of the second ramp.

Based on the geometric certainties of the pyramid, the second maze should have been much shorter than the first. However, it seemed to take just as long to find the exit as it had in the first set of twisting passages. When my eyes had once again adjusted to the light, I was dumbfounded to find myself leaving the maze by way of the exact same portal I had so recently exited at the bottom of the second ramp.

I tried the procedure again, this time with my left hand, but the attempt produced identical results. Quite baffled and not a little perturbed, I tried once more, this time alternating hands whenever I came to a turn. The technique yielded what I thought was a different route, but in the end, I still came out in the same place.

Feeling defeated, I resigned myself to descending the way I had come and finding another means of getting home. Knowing that I had come through the maze using my right hand, I reasoned that I should be able to make my way back to the first ramp by using my left. However, another plunge into the passage where my torch had gone out led me not back to ground level, but rather to another portal some half-way up the pyramid. I was not amused.

During the ensuing hour of exploration and experimentation, I established a working theory that re-entering a portal after having exited the pyramid usually—but maddeningly not always—led me incrementally farther up the structure, while climbing an exterior walkway and using its upper entrance invariably led me back to the bottom of said walkway. There did not, according to my research, seem to be any way to descend.

After fending off my rising dread that I'd never get back down from that damnable monument, I decided to use my newfound knowledge of the labyrinth's workings to summit the structure, where I would at the very least have the opportunity to signal for help.

The retreat-to-proceed strategy worked marvelously, eventually bringing me to a dead-end in the labyrinth where a ladder—felt but not seen—extended upward into a narrow, vertical shaft. The metal rungs grew warmer and rougher as I ascended, and upon unscrewing the hatch that I found at the top of the shaft, I emerged onto the pyramid's peak.

The air outside was crisp and refreshing, and I saw that I had completed my climb just in time to witness the sun beginning to set in a newly cloudless sky. I was also mollified to discover that the insufferable buzzing had stopped. The bright blue gazebo I had seen from the ground was actually quite large: it covered the entirety the pyramid's sizable plateau and housed an enormous, westward-facing marble statue of a man with a slight smile and curly locks of shortish hair who wore a reasonable approximation of Greek garb and sat on a throne made of variously sized geodesic spheres. I wondered if the statue had been added at some point substantially after the main structure's completion, as it was in superb condition relative to the rest of the pyramid; the only indication that the statue might not have been new was the fact that both of its hands were missing. Upon closer inspection, I noticed that the clean cut at the wrist of each of arm was weathered identically to the rest of the statue, which made me question whether the figure had ever had any hands at all.

As beautiful as the view was and as intriguing as I found the statue, I had no more desire to camp in the gazebo than in the woods. Exhausted from the climb and in dire need of a new plan, I looked for a place to sit down: the benches around the perimeter of the gazebo didn't look particularly comfortable, and the statue's lap was just out of easy reach, so I opted to straddle one of its huge, sandaled feet and recline against its toga-draped shin. My joy at being able to massage my swollen legs was soon supplanted by alarm as the colossal stone foot beneath me began to move. The marble giant drew itself up to full height, and my bowels prepared to evacuate as the figure craned down to stare me in the face.

"What seems to be the trouble?" the statue asked jovially.

Having narrowly retained my continence and struggling to find my voice, I somehow stammered out an answer about being lost and trying to use the pyramid to find my way home.

"Of course! I'd be glad to point you in the right direction," the statue offered. "Won't you stay, though? It gets dreadfully dull here on my own. I had this pavilion installed so I could sit and enjoy the sunsets, but it's been less enjoyable than I'd hoped without any company. I was just about to put the kettle on—can I interest you in a cup of tea?"

I had relapsed into a speechless daze, and it took me a few moments to process the giant's entreatment. When I realized that my silence likely seemed impolite, I regathered my wits and indicated that tea would be lovely. I then asked the statue who he was.

"How rude of me!" the statue exclaimed. "Please, call me Nash. Most people do."

I told him I was pleased to make his acquaintance and then clarified that I had meant to ask who he was in a historical sense and why the pyramid had been built in his honor.

"Ah, I think I see what you're getting at," Nash said with a dawning look. "I'm not the ghost of the person depicted by this statue, if that's what you mean. I simply inhabit this monument, and I'm much, much older than anything your kind has any history of. I'm using the statue because it would be a bit bizarre for the building itself or a being composed primarily of energy to talk to you like this, wouldn't it? I can change over if you like. It wouldn't be any trouble."

Trying to contain my excitement at the discovery of what I suspected to be extraterrestrial life, I said that a change wouldn't be necessary and asked Nash if he could confirm that he was an alien.

"I suppose I would be to you, wouldn't I?" he said. "There's a thought."

Though a million other questions probably should have taken precedence, for some reason I kept coming back to the creature's name. I told him that it was quite curious for an alien being to have a name as familiar as Nash.

"Oh, no," he corrected me, "my name isn't actually *Nash*. I'm afraid you wouldn't be able to pronounce my true name."

Slightly confused, I asked if Nash was his nickname.

"No, it's my Nash-name," he said. "It's just what I call myself here. I like others to call me that, too."

I tried not to be too miffed at this response and asked if he had just picked the name out for himself.

"Well, lots of people get to pick out their names, don't they?" he replied. "There's nothing so odd about that."

I told him I supposed that was true. I then asked him what had prompted him to pick "Nash".

"Nash is a cool name," he said and—seeming to think that this was explanation enough—turned away to prepare the tea.

As we sipped at our Darjeeling and watched the sun continue its retreat, I attempted to make sense of what was clearly an absurd situation. At some point, I gave up on the effort and simply enjoyed what I had to admit was an objectively lovely time.

"You're very lucky to have been chosen," Nash intimated after we had set our cups down. "My pyramid only appears to those worthy of its secrets."

After swallowing a bite of tea biscuit, I asked him how it was that I'd been deemed worthy.

"Oh, I don't know. You seemed like a nice enough chap," Nash responded moonily. "And as I said, it was getting awfully boring out here. I've been cooped up all week trying to deal with some moisture issues I've been having in the crypt. I can't stand being cooped up."

While we were on the subject, I took the opportunity to ask Nash about the pyramid's purpose and how he had come to inhabit the place.

"It's a funny story, actually," he said in a way that sounded rather well-rehearsed, "I was on my way to the adjacent arm of this galaxy when I crash-landed on account of a faulty pulse drive, which was further damaged upon impact. The locals found the wreckage, and after a number of sectarian wars were fought over their beliefs about its provenance, enough of them had died for them to settle on the notion that the ship was the steed of their sky god. I was the god in that equation, in case that wasn't clear," he said, continuing only after I'd nodded my acknowledgment. "They spent several generations building this shrine, which took my spacecraft as a sort of foundation. The energy leaking from the drive's core imbued the workers with what amounted to superhuman abilities, and they built all of this with nothing more than hand tools. Can you believe that? Amazing stuff. Unfortunately, the workers also went completely mad and died within about a month of sustained exposure. That didn't seem to matter to them, though. If there's one thing you can count on with humans, it's that they always want to be something they're not. That's probably why they were so eager to worship me, because I certainly didn't ask them to. Would have been a bit gauche, don't you think?"

I told him that our views on etiquette sounded similar.

"You should have seen how eager those people were to queue. At first, I was taken aback at how quickly the teams who perished were replaced by new volunteers, but I soon realized that they viewed the powers as a transformative blessing which apparently outweighed all the insanity and melting to death. On account of the madness, they did tend to get a bit haphazard in their work toward the end of any given group's service. I considered fixing their mistakes myself a few times, but I didn't want to come off as a meddler or risk offending them. They finished the project in their own time, and in celebration, I gave them the run of the place while I went on a short holiday. I don't think they heeded my warnings about not hanging around for too long at any one time, because when I came back, I found the place completely deserted. No idea where they went."

I asked what he'd been doing since the fanatics had disappeared.

"I've kept busy, for the most part. For a while, the occasional traveler would happen through and provide some company, but they grew to be few and far between as the years went by. You're the first visitor I've had in ages. I tried giving your predecessors powers as parting gifts by dosing them deliberately, but the early attempts didn't work out all that well," he said, gesturing to a jumble of faintly glowing bones jammed into the rafters of the gazebo. "I tend to fall behind on my housekeeping when no one comes around. It's a habit I'm trying to break." I must have worn my botheration on my sleeve, because Nash hastily added, "Oh, don't worry. You're in no danger. I was able to seal the malfunctioning drive, by and large. I also dialed the dosage in properly—the two guests I had immediately before you showed no ill effects after they received their powers. There are a few lingering, environmental effects of the core leak, but I find that they're fairly benign and sporadic. You must have noticed that awful noise and the difficulties in the maze, no?"

I said that I had and followed up by asking what the catch was if madness and death were no longer supposed to be a concern with regard to the powers.

"Right. Well, it seems that historically—here and elsewhere—there are rules to govern this kind of thing. There's a certain amount of power, and a responsibility which goes along with that power, and on like that," he said, his phantom hands following his words in hopping arcs as they went left to right. "In this case, you get one specific power—only one, on account of the lowered dosage—and it can be just about anything you can imagine, but there's the stipulation that you have to take the oath. With that in mind—" he said, raising his arms in an impressive manner, "do you swear to uphold the just and the true, to be the defender of the downtrodden and the weak, and to live the rest of your life as a shield against tyranny and oppression?"

I vacillated and told him that while it sounded like an amazing opportunity, I hadn't foreseen having to make a snap decision of such magnitude. I asked if I might possibly be able to sleep on it, citing the exceptionally long day I'd had as grounds for the reprieve.

"This is a first," he said, clearly crestfallen as his arms came to rest on the throne again. "No one has ever turned down the offer."

I reiterated that it wasn't a hard "no" and that I simply wanted a little more time to consider the proposition.

"I'm actually quite busy over the next few days," Nash answered after clicking his marble teeth together a number of times. "I have to be at the annual conference for energy beings who inhabit monuments." He grew silent for a time before piping back up. "You know what? Sod it. I'll just waive that part of the initiation. It's not like anyone ever enforces the oath, anyway. So—assuming there are no strings attached—what do you say?"

I said yes.

"Great! Glad to hear it," he said as his stony smile returned. "Now, there's just the matter of choosing how you'd like to be enhanced."

After a few moments' consideration, I specified the power I thought most useful.

"Interesting," he said, stroking his chin with the air at the end of his wrist. "Very interesting. You're a clever one, aren't you? I thought you might be." He stood up again and waved a stump over his throne, which consequently levitated a few inches off the ground and hovered over to one side, revealing a wide, cylindrical shaft that descended into the belly of the pyramid. "Well, a deal is a deal," Nash said, inclining his head toward the shaft and extending an invisible hand in my direction. "Shall we begin?"

The Other Side of the Mountain

There is a lowness, a stagnation. Being so little for so long,
being unmoved.
Cool, then frost. A hardening with the chill;
contraction without, expansion within. Clouded contents
beneath a glassy surface.

Waiting. Still waiting in the cold. Waiting in fading light
and lingering night. Waiting forever.
The sun extends its stay by day. Cold abates, only just.
Cracks in the ice.

A trickle of long-lost identity down the slope, from above.
A trickle becomes a stream, a stream a torrent.
There is fulfillment, a crispness. Being whole, being
new and clean.

Warm rain brings a sense of green. Rising.
The edge is reached—brimmed banks are no match for a
flood. A cascade of self rushes away,
disappears farther downhill.
The loss is felt deeply.

Exhalation

The Small Ones die so quickly! They breathe so frantic rapid, and use up all their Respirations at once. And because life is so short, do as you please. Never mind what the Large Ones say, never mind, should you even hear. The Large Ones die later, everyone knows. They move slower, too, and breathe in lazy waves, doled at glacial pace, a thousand turns of the Star. But does not every creature, great and small, have the same number? Respirations, of course. In and out! In and out! And is every creature not just the same as the others—maybe larger than, maybe smaller than—but the same in form, the same in function? And all of them living on the Largest One's back? The Large Ones breathe slow, and the Small Ones breathe fast, and all stop breathing when they reach the last.

But indeed they all die—some sooner than, some later than—and nothing can hold them on. All die, and each sounds the Rasp at the end, when vitalities fail, vivacious collapse. The Rasp of the Small is a buzz, a chirp. It is gone before it is heard, almost, and leaves no echo behind. The Rasp of the Large is a boulder down the mountain, massive. Crack! Crack! Crack! And echoes on forever.

The Large Ones noticed firstly, their memories long, eyes fixed far away, that the Smallest Ones began to die, and not come back. For the currents had slowed, and converged no more, and brought no Small Ones together. And they—the Small!—breathed so hectic free, swarming none the wiser. And they—the Large!—loosed warning down the chain, and worried of the end, befretted Exhalation. For they knew the Largest One was just the same as the others—maybe larger than—and must sometime reach its Rasp. They knew they must leave its back, and find another place to go on, but they moved too slow, and could not bring the change themselves. And they were wise to worry, and shrewd to fret, for the Small Ones could not hear above the din, their buzzing Rasp, and reveled in doing nothing.

And so the Smallest were rasped and gone, and the Ones larger than they—only just!—grew hungry and weak, and too died without coming back. And on it went, each withered and died and did not come back, until none but the Large Ones were left.

And now they cannot move to save, they can only

CRACK!

huddle close and watch, and listen as

CRACK!

the end comes, arrives before

CRACK!

they can even

The Holdout

Chrysalis was the place to be. Then again, there was nowhere else to go.

The result of centuries of research and development, the city was a beacon of scientific achievement and a testament to the potential of mankind. Of course, human endeavor alone had proved insufficient in realizing the founders' dreams, and the arrival of the Wanderers and their Othering technology had been instrumental in bridging the gaps in humanity's collective knowledge.

The streets and skies had grown empty in step with the implementation of the Wanderers' gift to the Chrysalians; the warpshift relocation that Othering made possible had obviated the need for most of the slow and inefficient modes of transportation which had preceded it. What remained to the few observers with high enough security clearance to be outdoors was an unobstructed skyline so complex and delicate that even its most hyperbolic description rang hollow; the gleaming spires and hovering conduit spheres of the last bastion of civilization could be seen for hundreds of miles.

Two such observers stood alone atop the easterly wall, inured to the thunderous vibrations below their feet—the titanic cylindrical towers which comprised the wall elsewhere along the city's perimeter were tunneling, as they did any time the population grew too dense. Soon, the columns would re-emerge from the brittle earth, extending the borders of the metropolis to afford its denizens the comfortable living space to which they had become accustomed.

Milli looked out from her elevated vantage point, her eyes scanning the sun-scorched wasteland that encircled the city. "Look at them," she whispered as she motioned to the distant figures scrabbling in the dust; she held them in her augmented gaze as she reached for her older brother's hand. "That used to be us."

Jairo's hand was cold to the touch; he'd opted for a GripAug installation the month before. "Good thing it's not anymore," he scowled as his hand twitched into a fist, narrowly missing Milli's fingers. Jairo kept his eyes fixed on the far-off wretches as he spat over the edge of the wall; Milli suspected he was aiming for the poor creatures, but they were so far away that she was forced to take it as a symbolic gesture. She leaned forward to watch the globule trace a spasmodic trajectory down to the ground but then flinched at an unexpected jab in her side. "We need to go," Jairo intoned as he withdrew his thumb from his sister's ribs. "It's only your second month. The captain won't be amused if she hears you're already showing up late."

The siblings descended from the battlement in silence, with the low thrum of the lift nearly lulling Milli to sleep. She'd been dosing herself with SomniRite to combat the sleepless nights the new job had been causing her, but the pill-induced torpor was full of visions and far from restful.

Jairo must have seen her attempt at covering a yawn, because he cleared his throat the way he did whenever he disapproved of something. Milli's tender flank protested as she snapped to attention; she imagined her brother would have been pleased to know that at least some of her new training was putting down roots.

Before long, they reached ground level and hustled along the rows of towering photofarms that lined the route to the nearest shiftgate. Milli knew it was as far as they'd go together. "Don't wait up," Jairo said as they approached the portal. "After patrol, we have to demolish a new set of tunnels the sensors picked up last week, so I won't be off duty until nine at the earliest. The team is probably going to want to blow off some steam afterward." He gave his sister's arm a squeeze, slightly too hard, before stepping through the gate and vanishing. Milli was relieved to think that she might be asleep before Jairo got home. She loved her brother, but he was a severe man. The trait was more pronounced when he drank.

Jairo's temperament was well-suited to his job in Chrysalis. He had always demonstrated a great love for the institution of authority, and as a mid-rank officer in the government's law enforcement arm, he'd found the kind of rigid hierarchy and binary ethics he craved. While agents of his kind were officially called Keepers of Public Order, common vernacular had another label for them, derived from their preferred method of securing compliance from unruly citizens: the Stunners commanded nearly universal fear and respect from the civilians under their purview.

In the eyes of some Chrysalians, there were no darker parts of the city; such citizens often questioned the necessity of a policing body altogether. The fact of the matter was that Chrysalis, while unquestionably a technological utopia, was nevertheless populated by imperfect beings. Although the particulars of law enforcement had certainly changed in the decades since the city was sealed to the outside world, the Stunners still had plenty to do; collapsing tunnels and repelling incursions from the wastelands took up the bulk of their time, but Chrysalis also had its fair share of homegrown criminals. On the one hand, vices such as theft and rape had practically disappeared, owing to Othering's saturation of the pleasure market. On the other, on-tap gratification didn't do much to stem the indiscretion of murder. There were simply too many reasons to want to kill someone.

Notwithstanding the yellowish bruise forming below her left breast, Milli was thankful of her brother's indelicate reminder about the time; she had to rush to get skinned up for duty and just barely made it into the briefing room before the tunnel sealed behind her. She'd heard stories from senior crew members about what happened to slackers who found themselves on the other side of that heavy door when the captain came through for inspection, and she was in no hurry to experience it for herself.

Though she hadn't quite caught her breath by the time it was her turn to pass muster, Milli stood rigidly and put on her most serious face; she was fairly sure that everyone could hear her nose whistling with each breath, but the captain took only a little longer in looking her over than she usually did, and in the end her only remark was that Milli's insignia was slightly askew.

In the short time that she'd known her commanding officer, Milli had already developed a profound reverence for the woman. The captain was a strong and serious leader, and the Collectors under her command harbored a fierce loyalty to her. She kept her personal life to herself, though, and

Milli had never seen her fraternize: not with anyone outside of duty and certainly not with her subordinates. Some interpreted the captain's behavior as aloof or standoffish, but Milli saw it as self-reliance, if a little myopic at times. Whereas other female civil servants often resorted to classical tactics of advancement in what was still very much a boys' club, the captain had been promoted on merit alone. Milli imagined there was a healthy portion of resentment at the root of the other women's contempt for her boss.

Though the captain was invariably dispassionate in carrying out her duty, Milli thought she recognized a deep sort of sadness behind the woman's steely demeanor. She saw it only rarely—usually just after the last of the assignments, during the unguarded moment when the captain turned to withdraw to her quarters—but it was definitely there. She wished there were some way for her to communicate to the captain that she knew the feeling.

Milli's heart rate had nearly returned to normal by the time Brial was up for inspection; as group leader, he was always last to face the captain's scrutiny. Many on the crew saw the young Collector as the obvious choice to succeed the captain when she came up for retirement at the end of the decade. Others, including Milli, were wary of his unchecked ambition; he regularly set new records for collection rates and had even memorized the entire regulatory codex, a feat which no one apart from the captain could claim to have accomplished. He was also completely full of himself. Unfortunately, nobody could argue that his hubris wasn't warranted.

"Flawless as usual, group leader," the captain said, nodding matter-of-factly at Brial, who fought valiantly to hold in a smirk until she had turned away. Milli felt her lips twist into an unattractive shape.

With inspection over, the captain segued to the morning's briefing. As Milli had already heard from her brother, a number of new incursion tunnels had been discovered in the buffer zone around the city. The Collectors wouldn't have to deal with the problem themselves, but the captain wanted them to be aware of the demolition work that Public Order would be doing over the course of the coming days; the reverberations from a subterranean collapse could easily be mistaken for the approach of one of the sandstorms that frequently barreled through the region. While these "scours" posed little threat to the city itself, anything beyond the protection of the Othering field was extremely vulnerable; the storms were powerful enough to carry a collection skid for several miles and could easily breach a HazSkin before abrading flesh down to the bone.

When the captain had finished, she saluted the group and handed control of the proceedings over to Brial, who immediately started barking orders and rattling off team assignments. Milli's team was tasked with clearing the northeastern quadrant, where they'd likely visit the Holdout settlement she and Jairo had seen earlier that morning. While the rest of her teammates were responsible for prepping the skid for the day's excursion, Milli was tasked with procuring the reserve HazSkins and SlingShock weapons they would need. After filing out of the briefing room behind the others in the group, she broke off and shuffled down the narrow corridor that led to central supply.

There were at least a dozen people waiting to get into the depot when Milli arrived, and the one-in, one-out policy meant that she had a particularly long wait ahead of her. Even though it would have made everyone's lives a lot easier if they'd been allowed to warpshift mission-critical equipment directly to their teams, concerns about hack-ins meant that shiftgates weren't permitted anywhere inside of secure areas. Controlled goods like HazSkins and SlingShock units weren't cleared for shifting anyway, regardless of the end-to-end security, which meant that Milli and anyone else with official need of such items had to go pick up the gear in person.

Milli fell into line behind a pair of young servicemen, whom she didn't immediately recognize as Criss and Tilger; the two had been in her basic training unit before being recruited by the Department of Innovation and the Journalistic Authority, respectively. She was about to strike up a conversation, but then she remembered the last interaction she'd had with Tilger.

"The Holdouts committed their crimes generations ago," Milli had argued. "Doesn't the fact that they keep trying to get into the city say that maybe they've seen the error of their ways? I just think it might be time to reassess our policy of keeping them out at all costs."

"They had their choice to make, and they chose to be dead weight," Tilger had retorted. "We had to cut them loose and move on for the good of the species. And if I didn't know any better, I'd say you sounded like an enemy of progress."

Milli hadn't broached subjects of substance with anyone since—the last thing she wanted was to wind up on the List. Public servants weren't allowed to diverge from party dogma when it came to the Holdouts, even though the ruling class tolerated the sporadic civilian protests held by the city's token number of sympathizers. Most citizens were too contented to join the ranks of the conscientious anyway, which made it easy for the technocrats to paint the movement as a fringe group made up of those outside the contours of respectable credibility. The gambit worked beautifully.

Still, not being able to speak her mind didn't change the way Milli felt about the situation. Although the Chrysalians had never been outright aggressors, they didn't shy away from using force to keep the Holdouts at arm's length. The mile-wide area of denial that ringed the city was guarded by an array of automated sentry turrets, and because the New Constitution's prohibition on summary execution didn't extend to the Holdouts, the first iteration of the border protection system came to be known as the Meatgrinder. In an effort to quell the bleeding hearts' outrage at the reports of carnage beyond the wall, the turrets were eventually redesigned to be "less-lethal", which was a shrewd way of saying that they killed marginally fewer targets than they would have with live ammunition. The stasis gel rounds fired by the revamped turrets were designed to immobilize their targets for twelve hours; the incapacitation was meant to act as a deterrent without putting the captive in danger of starvation or dehydration. Unfortunately for the Holdouts, the system's survivability models didn't account for the effects of a scour on targets unlucky enough to be trapped in its path.

Milli had seen the aftermath of that particular brand of misfortune. Usually, the only thing the Collectors found after a Holdout had been caught in a scour was a desiccated husk of leathery skin and lightened bones, though sometimes the extremities that had been sealed in gel were left partially intact. Milli thought this was likely cold comfort to the victims' family and friends, who were often in the tragic position of being unable to help their loved ones for fear of being killed themselves.

Whenever the Collectors reached one of the settlements, they presented the bodies of the dead with as much humility as could be mustered after a day of working in the blistering heat. While there was no statutory compulsion to treat the Holdouts with kindness, there was definitely a pragmatic reason to do so. The alternative had already been tested: the task of clearing the area of denial was originally assigned to an army of drones, but it was soon made clear that the Holdouts didn't appreciate the remains of their deceased being unceremoniously dumped in their encampments by faceless body bins; their dismay had translated into a marked increase in infiltration attempts on the city and had ultimately led to the creation of the Collector program in its current form. There was a begrudging gratefulness in the Holdouts' eyes when the Collectors came to call, but there was still suspicion and no small measure of anger, as well. Milli could hardly blame them.

Some of the other Collectors complained of difficulty in differentiating the Holdouts from one another, saying that the scavengers all started to look the same after a while. This couldn't have been farther from the truth for Milli. Brought to unbidden life in her SomniRite-fueled dreams, every detail of every one of their squalid faces was embossed in her memory. One face, more than any other, was responsible for the bags under her eyes and the ache in her heart. It belonged to a little girl she had seen in the southwest quadrant's secondary settlement. The child had been stricken with a disfiguring disease, long since eradicated in Chrysalis, which had twisted and distended her features into a mask that was at once horrifying and pitiable. Of course, the Chrysalians had the necessary vaccine in ample supply, but the ImmunoPak cartridges used an Othering-based delivery method to administer the dose, and there was no political will to hand the tech over to the Holdouts. The girl's face was emblematic of all the things Milli feared she couldn't change; she saw the failings of mankind in that face, born of a callousness that no amount of progress could subdue.

Milli had been told that there was no stopping the march of progress. Thankfully, the same was true of the line in front of the supply depot; Criss and Tilger were nowhere to be seen, which meant that she would be the next one in.

The depot guard, Lynis, was preoccupied with reading something over his OptiLink when Milli inserted her procurement chip into the console next to his booth. He simply sat there and stared off into space, his eyes tracking slowly from left to right before snapping back to their initial position and starting over again.

"Stand on the mark. Recite your name and rank," Lynis said with rote disinterest, still reading as the security module's sensor conduit emerged from a panel above Milli's head. "Make sure your face isn't obstructed."

Milli did as she was told, waiting as the slim metal serpent above her twisted and curled before freezing a few feet in front of her nose. The aperture at the end of the articulated arm dilated, and a sensation of prickling warmth washed over her face. The display in front of Lynis bathed him in green; he flicked his eyes down just long enough to confirm the system message before returning to his invisible literature.

"Try to be quick about it," Lynis said to the empty space in front of him. "It's going to be a zoo today."

As she walked along countless aisles of devices whose purposes were beyond her ken, Milli tried to ward off the unease that accompanied each of her trips into the depot. Like so many other things in the city, the place had been a gift from the Wanderers, and it was clear that they'd had efficiency in mind when they designed it. It was not clear, however, that humans had also been in mind at the time. The dimensions and layout of everything in the warehouse were off by just enough that every interaction was unintuitive; it evoked the unshakeable feeling of being a stranger in one's own home.

When she came to a row of shelves laden with SlingShock units, Milli kept walking. The weapons required a secondary biometric scan, and the crates were considerably heavier than those of the HazSkins, so she usually saved herself some trouble by picking them up on the way out. She'd yet to use one of the weapons out in the field, and she had never seen a live target hit with a shock round, but Jairo had told her plenty of stories. It sounded terrible. It also sounded better than the way things had been before.

The HazSkins were something with which she was much more familiar. The one she was currently wearing had her name etched into the space above her heart, and it fit her so well that she hardly noticed she was wearing anything at all. The reserves stacked on the shelf in front of her were all blanks, but the integrated autosizing feature ensured that anyone on the team would be able to wear them. Milli thought about the fact that the Holdouts still had to make their clothing on an individual basis, with varying degrees of ill-fitting results. She came into regular contact with the material in bringing the lost souls back to their families, and she relished the visceral feeling of its weave against the pads of her fingers. It was beautiful, indurable stuff which had no analogue in the world behind the wall, and she knew there was something woven into its fibers that the people of Chrysalis had lost.

She removed one of the HazSkins from its container, and the mercurial fabric poured through her fingers as she let it fall from one palm to the other. It was an ingenious invention, and the effect was mesmerizing, but it did not make her feel. She let the garment slip to the floor, where it pooled into a perfect circle. The inkling of a plan that had been swelling in her subconscious over the preceding weeks had finally exploded, and her legs were already carrying her to other end of the depot before her mind caught up with what had been set into motion.

Several minutes later, the door of the medical storage room sighed open behind her, casting a net of cool blue light across her back and throwing her kneeling silhouette onto the wall in front of her. Something told her to run, but her hands ignored the urge and continued in their flurried work, grabbing as many ImmunoPaks as they possibly could and stuffing them into the satchel she'd brought for the other supplies. As a heavy shadow filled the room, she envisioned the little girl's face and thought of all the good she could have done had she only had a little more time. The hair on the back of her neck stood on end, and she stifled a scream as the flesh of her right shoulder yielded under the weight of cold, inexorable fingers.

———

They scar her face to match their own, but her eyes are still too bright. There's nothing to do for that but wait.

She digs her unaccustomed hands raw in the parched earth, struggling to keep up with the harder creatures that surround her. The blurred behemoth on the horizon draws nearer by the minute, and the air hangs silent and still amidst the dust dwellers. The coming storm will be the exile's first; she is wise to be afraid. Hands reach in from all sides, and she flinches— not at the offer of help, but at the sudden return of the pain burning in her side.

Miles away, a lone figure watches from a high and gleaming place.

A growing wall divides them.

Open to Interpretation:
The Curse of The Vague

Hi, and welcome to your adventure story. For the duration of the tale, I'll be your narrator, guide, and moral compass, among other things. What? Lover? Take it easy, friend—we just met. We'll talk, though.

Before we begin, please take the time to mark this location. We have a long journey ahead of us, and it would be a shame if you couldn't find your way home in the off-chance things take a left turn. Got it? Good.

We can jump into the fray in just a few moments, but we need to take care of one last little thing before we do. First, please choose your gender. It doesn't make any real difference for the story. I just want to see how well you can follow directions.

CHOOSE!

A) I'm a dude, bro. I want to be male. (Go to 1)

B) I'm a sister, sister. Make me female. (Go to 1)

C) Screw you. You can't cram me into one of your outdated, rigid gender roles. I'm a person—it's irrelevant what kind of genitalia I have. Also, screw you for making "female" second on the list. (Go to 23)

1

Great work. Looks like you have the basic skill set needed to proceed with your quest (even if you're one of those who took an extra step or two to get here). Let's get started.

Ahem.

Years after your adventure began and many miles from home, you stand at the base of the Flaming Spire. You've been climbing for days to reach this point; perched high on a snowy mountain peak, the stronghold soars above you, carving a great wound in the clear summer sky and looming large over the deep and fertile river valley below. Swooping, razor-edged volcanic glass, claret in color, runs around the outside of the fortress in tight spirals, lending the tower its infernal appearance and making an exterior ascent all but impossible. Your arch-nemesis, The Vague, awaits your arrival at the top of the tower. This is a showdown which has been a *really* long time coming. Seriously, ages. You're super excited about it.

You do a lap around the base of the tower to evaluate possible angles of attack. It appears, however, that the only entrance at ground level is a curiously normal-sized wooden door on the valley side of the spire. The door is sturdily built and secured with a heavy but simple lock. You're a little baffled, but one thing is certain: you need to get inside and start the climb to final combat.

What do you do?

A) No time to waste. I want to break down the door—it'll give me a chance to try out my new Kickin' Boots™ (Go to 20)

B) I'm a good listener and slick with a pick. Let's have a quick eavesdrop, then break in, sneaky-like. (Go to 14)

C) I'll just climb in through the nearest window—it's only about thirty feet above my head. (Go to 7)

2

You wait until the guards are within easy earshot and then launch your verbal chicanery. "Look Over There!" you yell in the most convincing way you can, with wide eyes and pointing and everything. The three guards all turn their heads so quickly that they veer into one another, trip, and impale themselves on each other's weapons. Huh. Call that one a freebie, I guess. Don't let it make you complacent, though. I'm serious. There are totally going to be more difficult things to deal with in this tower than these guys—you watch.

You stroll past the jumble of dead meatheads and toward the back of the hall; it turns out there are exactly two ways out of this room. Okay, three, if you count the door you just came in through, but that would be a bit silly, don't you think? After all that? Let's focus on moving forward. There are two stone arches, one to the left and one to the right. Both lead to seemingly identical stairways which spiral upward, presumably to the next floor of the tower.

Which path do you want to take?

A) I'll take the path to the right. (Go to 8)

B) Let's go left. (Go to 12)

3

Being careful not to nudge or bump any of the finely tuned equipment in the room, you don the blackout lenses, cross your fingers, and pull the lever.

An array of mirrored panels all around the room swing open simultaneously, filling the chamber with the dazzling light of the afternoon sun. You're certainly glad that you have the spectacles, as the light in the room is so hot and bright that you can feel your skin start to sizzle. Every bit of sunlight in the room finds its way to the lens on the pedestal, which, in turn, is now blasting the powerful beam of collected energy down the hallway. You find a cool spot in the corner near the floor, huddle down, and watch the action through the spaces between your fingers.

At first, you think nothing is happening. After a brief pause, though, you hear a symphony of inhuman screaming and thrashing from the hallway— a ferocious something-or-other sounds to be having a very nasty time in there. The din in the passageway culminates in a loud *splat*, followed by silence. You move the lever back to its original position, closing the panels and cutting off the supply of sunlight to the lens. You remove the shades and wait for a few minutes while your eyes adjust; when they have, you head to the center of the room to establish what's happened.

The lens, which you thought might be useful to you later, has a number of large cracks running through its center. It seems the intense heat from the light which was focused on the lens has ruined it. You try to examine the impressive piece of optics to see if it might be salvageable, but it falls apart in your hands. So, no lens.

You walk down the exit hallway, which is now lit well enough to negotiate with ease: there is a trough of burning oil running along the wall near the ceiling which must have ignited when you used the light cannon. About thirty feet along the passage, there is closed steel door connected to a very familiar looking linkage; on the floor in front of the door, you find a smoldering pile of rags with a chain sitting on it. There is iridescent slime coating the floor and dripping from the walls and ceiling—the stuff looks like it exploded outward from the pile of rags. After a bit of headscratching and digging in your mental vaults, you postulate that the beam of light which was fired down the hallway must have killed some kind of creature which was released from its cell when the panels were opened in the main chamber. Based on the rags and chain, you venture a guess that it was a dreaded Spectral Painbeast: a semi-living netherworld monster which is immune to everything but magic and which garners sustenance from human suffering. You're really glad you didn't have to see it up close. It probably would have been scary. You also recall that Painbeasts can't be killed—you can just dispel them for a while. You can't remember how long it takes them to reconstitute themselves (you skipped that day of hero school to see the circus and missed the second part of the lesson on nether-beasts), so you decide it would probably be best to step lively.

You hurry to the end of the hall, where you find a wooden gate and a small iron panel on the wall with a button labeled "UP". You push the button, and the gate retracts into the wall to the right, revealing a small metal chamber; the space is just big enough for a few people your size to stand in. You step into the chamber and find another panel—this one says "Service Lift 1" and is outfitted with a row of buttons. They are labeled as follows:

Floors 4-7: Maintenance *(please use maintenance key for access)*

Floor 8: Treasure Room *(whosoever emerges alive shall enjoy wealth beyond measure)*

Floor 9: Troll Reducer Storage *(access from service lift 2 <u>only</u>, due to construction work)*

Floor 10: Roof Level & Panorama Deck *(binoculars available at reception)*

Did you find a key for the maintenance department anywhere? I think one of those guards at the beginning had a keyring. What do you mean, you didn't check? What do you mean, because I didn't tell you to? You can do some things on your own, you know. Yes, I thought about it then. Yes, I suppose I could have suggested it in a way that wouldn't have broken the rules. Okay. OKAY. You're right. This one's on me, I'll own it. But, come on, lighten up a bit. There was probably nothing interesting on those floors anyway. I mean, maintenance? *BOR*-ing, right? Yeah, that would have been boring.

The button for the eighth floor doesn't work, but there is a star-shaped indentation right next to it. You think you might have something in your pack which would fit in there, but you'll have to check.

The ninth floor button has been taped over. You're not quite sure what "tape" is, but there it is. In any case, you can't go to floor nine.

Of course, you could just push the button for ten, go straight up to the roof and have it out with The Vague. That is why you're here after all, isn't it?

So, where do you want to go?

A) I'm tired of dicking around. Let's go fight The Vague. (Go to 13)

B) I want to swim in a sea of gold. Let's take the lift to the Treasure Room. *You need to have the special item from text 23 to take this path. You know who you are, Ballsy.* (Go to 15)

4

Sorry if this seems like a rude question, but do you think you might have an attention problem? Really, I'm asking. The Vague *just* used a spell to disarm you, and that one worked. I mean, I guess he could have used magnets or something, but that's kind of beside the point. The point is that he can back up his threats. Also, he's managed to get himself up to the top of this tower, which you just had a really hard time doing yourself. Oh, and the burning, evil crystal around his neck—that thing looks like it could be legit. I'm pretty sure he used it to possess that kid. No, I'm not trying to tell you what to do. No, of course! Of course you can do it your way, you can do it any way you want. I'm not trying to push. Go ahead, do it your way.

All I'm saying is that I would not have bet the way you just did, given the information we have on hand. There, I'm done.

So, here's how things go down: however The Vague managed that fireball, it's real. Your headlong dash into peril certainly makes you look the part of the hero. The flesh melting from your face, however, undoes any positive impression you might have been making. As the mystic fire consumes the rest of your body, you wonder where it all went wrong. You think, "Maybe I should have listened more closely to my friends." Shut up, that's exactly what you think as you're dying. That's your last thought. Then you die.

After the few lingering cinders are carried away on the wind, all that's left of you is a lightly charred right hand, the fingertips of which are gently grasping the hem of The Vague's satin robes. After he's had a good, hard laugh (his ribs are going to hurt for the rest of the day), The Vague takes the hand home with him and has it made into a backscratcher. He uses it on a fairly regular basis these days.

Sometimes he uses it on his butt.

I was really rooting for you, friend. Too bad you choked at the end.

(Go back to 1)

5

Your sword flashes out of its scabbard, severing the rope from its anchor on the wall and sending the chandelier plummeting. However, the guards see you do this—they do indeed look dumb, but they're not blind. Also, that chandelier is WAY up there, and it's taking longer than expected to fall. The guards move out of the way of the crashing ironwork and burning wax with time to spare; they continue marching in your direction.

You ask the guards if they'd like to talk about it, hoping that your sterling conversational skills might help you wriggle your way out of this jam. As the guards rip you limb from limb, you have the sneaking suspicion that no, they probably don't want to talk about it.

I'm pretty sure you're dead now. Let me check...yeah, yep. You're dead. Door nail.

(Go back to 1)

6

You use the unconscious child as a human shield. *YOU USE THE UNCONSCIOUS CHILD AS A HUMAN SHIELD?* Are you kidding me? Are you really going to make me narrate this? You're as bad as The Vague. Worse, maybe. You don't, I don't know, try to *deflect* the fireball, or *extinguish* it, or anything like that: you go straight for sacrificing the child. Oh, wait, sorry: first you bash the kid over the head, *then* you sacrifice him. I mean, come on. Sure, the little guy is messed up right now, but what if there's a way to save him? What if there's a cure or counterspell for whatever's wrong with him?

Ugh. Okay, fine.

As the child is consumed by the magical flames, his ashes fall into a sooty little pile, covering your boots. Those stains are definitely not going to come out. The repercussions of what you've just done race through your mind as your lift your eyes to meet The Vague's. As you search each other's faces, trying to make sense of the events of the last few minutes, you have the uncanny sensation of peering into a mirror.

"Welcome home, my friend," The Vague smiles warmly as he rushes to embrace you with open arms.

As the years go by, The Vague teaches you the intricacies of being a career villain; there are a surprising number of responsibilities and considerations which had never even occurred to you. Is it better to ransom a king's son or his favorite mistress? What if you have to go to the toilet, but you're right in the middle of giving a pre-battle pep talk to your orcish horde? Which robe material best conveys a sense of menace: satin, silk, or fur? It turns out that the answer to this last one depends on the season, actually, and is a bit counter-intuitive.

You help The Vague work on his confusing way of saying things. It's slow progress, but he does get better after a fashion—at one point, he even considers changing his name to The Only Sometimes Misunderstood. However, you and he both decide that "The Vague" has a better ring to it, so things stay as they are. Your partnership of darkness flourishes, and year by year, the terrifying shadow of your evil empire slowly envelops the globe...

You know what? I don't think I can do this anymore. I'm sorry, this just really isn't what I signed up for. I'm going to leave you two sociopaths to it. You deserve each other. No, really, you guys can sort yourselves out. I was really into narrating the story when you were still the hero and I knew where I stood, but this doesn't feel right. I'm washing my hands of this whole thing. I can't do it.

I just can't.

An End.

(But not the one I would have chosen for you.)

7

Did you not hear me? I just said the whole tower is covered in really, really sharp volcano glass. It's probably enchanted, too, I don't know. You can't climb it. Hey, no! Just, just...stop. Stop it. You're only going to cut your hands up worse than you already have. Please, go try something else. Humor me.

(Go back to 1)

8

As you exit the stairwell, you find that you have to squat to avoid scraping your head on the ceiling. The second floor of the tower consists of a long and low white marble hallway which leads to another ascending staircase. There is one expansion about halfway along the passage; in this domed chamber, you find a large, ornate altar with an inset golden sarcophagus, the lid of which is adorned with a life-sized depiction of some long-dead warrior king. The hands of the carved king are folded around the hilt of the most beautiful sword you've ever seen: precious stones of all kinds are set in every available surface of the silver guard, and the grip is wrapped in gold braiding. Bluish runes run along the entire length of the gleaming blade, which looks supremely sharp. Seriously, you could probably shave with this thing. It would be a little unwieldy, but you could totally do it.

You look down at your own sword, which you used to think was pretty nice. It's the first one you bought for yourself back when you first became a hero, after you'd gotten tired of using all the hand-me-downs. You'd saved for months to buy it, and you almost had to spend all of the money for mother's medicine when she contracted the pox, but she died too quickly for treatment, so you dodged that bullet. That sounded wrong; what I meant to say was that everything really sucked at the time and you were completely torn up, but that afterward, having a shiny new sword did make the coping process a little easier.

Your sword isn't the newest anymore. The pommel comes a little loose from time to time, and the leather grip could probably use replacing, but really, it's a good sword. It's worked perfectly well for all of the hero-type stuff you've ever had to do. Holds a nice edge, too. To be honest, you use it more like a tool than anything else, pounding and slashing and prying things that get in the way of your questing. You wonder if you would just wind up ruining the fancy sword if you did decide to take it.

Your eyes go back and forth from your sword to the king's for a while, eventually falling on the inscription at the base of the altar:

THE BATTLE FOR FYLESIA DID COME TO A CLOSE, AND VAELIR, SON OF VARKOTH AND KING OF THE KRAAL, DID RAISE HIS THONIAN BLADE TO SLAY THE DRAKKEN, RALJJ. AS MORTAL REVENGE, THE WOUNDED RALJJ DID PIERCE VAELIR'S KINGLY ARMOR WITH HIS WICKED TAIL, AND THE KING DID FALL ILL WITH POISON. THIRTY-THREE NIGHTS DID VAELIR ENDURE, AND DID EXCLAIM WITH HIS DYING BREATH:

DON'T TOUCH MY STUFF WHEN I'M DEAD, GUYS.

FOR REAL.

You realize that you should probably move along instead of hanging around in this tomb all day. What's it going to be?

A) I'll take the sword with me. It's much better than mine, and this stiff doesn't need it, anyway. (Go to 18)

B) I'm going to leave the sword and press on. I mean, there's a sign on the thing that says not to take it. (Go to 12)

9

You think the lens looks like it could be pretty dangerous, and you have a hunch that things are about to get toasty in here. You gingerly take the humming lens down from its pedestal and stow it, along with its little pillow, in your pack. Feeling a little more secure about the whole situation, you return to the wall, put on the protective glasses, and pull the lever.

The chamber does indeed get hot—and bright. Sunlight streams in from hundreds of panels which are now hanging open around the room; the remaining mirrors are all focusing the light onto the spot where the lens once sat. The focal point is so violently luminous that, even with the shaded lenses, you have to squint severely to keep your eyes from hurting.

Unfortunately, apart from the significant discomfort you've caused yourself, you're pretty sure you haven't achieved anything by activating this contraption. You realize now that the lens probably needs to be in position for this whole thing to work. However, putting it back right now is not an option: the supernova of sunlight on the pedestal is not going to let you anywhere near it, at least not with any of the water in your body left unboiled. You decide to shut it all down, replace the lens, and try again.

You're about to push the lever into its original position when you hear an ear-splitting, other-worldly shriek from the darkened hallway. A moment later, a creature emerges from the shadows and advances on your position with startling speed. The ragged cloth hanging from its ethereal form and the red-hot chain it drags behind it tell you that this can be only one kind of monster: a Spectral Painbeast. You now know why someone went through all the trouble of setting up this chamber: Spectral Painbeasts are incredibly ill-tempered and, on account of their nether-ness, unaffected by non-magical attacks. The lens was probably meant to shoot all that sunlight down the hallway and disintegrate the nasty bugger. Damn. Well, you're in for it now, buddy. These things really like to torture humans, so you might want to figure something out, quick.

Realizing that you don't have time to operate the lever twice before the monster is upon you, you scramble to put the lens back into place with things as they are. Unfortunately, it turns out that you can't reach the pedestal, on account of both the intense solar heat and the searing chain which the Painbeast has just whipped around your throat. It's also knocked your sunglasses off, blinding you in the process. Bonus. You clench your eyes shut and thrash around wildly for a few minutes, still trying to find somewhere useful to put the lens; the Painbeast torques the chain left and right and plays around with the amount of slack it gives your leash. At one point, it lets you get so close to the pedestal that you feel your upraised hands start to sizzle. Sensing that this might be your last chance to replace the lens and turn the tide, you lunge blindly toward the source of the heat. Your hands burst into flame and you drop the lens, which promptly shatters into a million pieces.

Your screams are a delight to the Painbeast, which takes the liberty of getting closer to its new pet—it pulls itself over to you via your chain leash, spreads your jaws as wide as they'll go, and crawls inside you. Taking control of your limbs, the monster puppets you around while you continue your full-throated wailing. Your legs kick and snap as it forces you to do a frantic jig all around the room, and it uses its control of your arms to make you gouge your own eyes out with your still-flaming thumbs. The mirrored walls of the room reflect the kaleidoscope of your demise back at you a thousand fold—you're thankful you're unable to see it. It sounds terrible.

Man. That was really, really unpleasant. Let's not do it again, eh?

You're dead, in case that wasn't clear.

(Go back to 1)

10

You skip the flashy stuff and hurl all of your ninja stars at once, aiming for the wooden rafters along the ceiling. Several rapid and satisfying *thunks* later, the shurikens ignite their collective payload, shattering the massive supports. The troll is completely unfazed by the subsequent hail of giant stones; it actually seems to enjoy it every time a boulder cracks it over the skull. The multitude of barrels which are falling from the room above, however, have a different effect on the monster.

As the barrels tumble and dash against the hard stone floor, they release huge plumes of purplish powder up into the air. The dust doesn't seem to do anything to you, apart from remind you very insistently of the smell of roasted garlic. The troll, on the other hand, has a much more adverse reaction to the pollutant and starts sneezing violently. Each time the troll sneezes, it shrinks to about half of its pre-sneeze size. Within a matter of fifteen seconds, the giant has shrunk to the size of a chipmunk, a change that does not discourage it from trying desperately to heft its still-giant club between sneezes.

You pick up the miniature troll, which continues to sneeze in little high-pitch squeaks. Even though it was just about to annihilate you a minute ago, you feel sorry for the tiny thing. Eventually—after all the dust has settled—it stops sneezing and just stares up at you, still a bit nonplussed on account of the role reversal, from the middle of your palm. You walk over to the exterior wall and put the creature up on the windowsill where it can get a nice view of the valley below. The troll gives you a thankful look with minuscule, watery eyes and then curls up in a spot of sun on the stone sill. You can hear it snoring gently as you navigate your way through the fallen rubble between you and treasure chest at the far end of the room.

The latch on the treasure chest is free of any locks—the person who put the treasure here must have figured that a lock would not be much of a deterrent to someone who had bested a Hypertroll. You're not complaining. You flip the latch upward, and with a little *creak,* the chest lid hovers open. Inside, you find not gold or jewels, but a small, plain key and an expertly smithed pewter hand mirror. The key, you surmise, is for the door leading back the elevator (*Found You*); you tuck it quickly away and refocus your attention on the finely made mirror. The intricacies of the metalwork leave you breathless—for a moment. Then, you think about all the grief you just went through to get this thing. "Wealth beyond measure", the sign said. Yeah, right. This thing, while nice, wouldn't fetch more than a few dozen kopeks at the bazaar.

You consider the mirror for a few minutes, and then a thought occurs to you. Thinking this might be one of those wish-granting or all-seeing mirrors, you try out all of the magical phrases and commands you've heard over the course of your travels. You think you see something stir in the mirror when you use "Sim, Sim, Salabim", but it turns out it was just a reflection of the micro-troll repositioning itself on the windowsill behind you. After about an hour of trying, you give up on the magic angle. Hate to say it, but it looks like this is just one of those symbolic treasures which are supposed to teach you a lesson. You know, like, "You were the treasure all along, you just never knew it," or some crap like that. Ah, well. At least the troll looks happy, right?

You would be justified in feeling cheated, but you always try to look on the bright side. It's still a pretty nice mirror, and you don't have one at home—you've been meaning to get one, as a matter of fact. At the very least, this will save you a trip to the mirror store. You tuck your prize into your pack, give the sleeping troll a goodbye pat on the head, and turn back to the lift.

(Go to 13)

11

You decide that a little demolition is in order. In one swift, fluid motion, you grab the explosive stars from their hiding place in your tunic and toss them with expert accuracy at the troll's feet. A split second later, the floor heaves, buckles and then collapses underneath the creature. The troll roars furiously as it falls into the purgatory that is the maintenance department.

The resulting void in the floor is well within your abilities *vis-a-vis* jumping over things; you could clear double this span in your sleep. So, without further ado, you bound gracefully over the chasm to claim your prize. You stick the landing and rub your hands together in anticipation of getting at that sweet, sweet treasure.

The troll's massive hand around your ankle makes you wonder why you didn't check to see if it could still reach you from down there. As the monster pulls you down off the ledge, you think that maybe it might have been better to forgo the treasure on this trip through the tower, you know, just focus on the "The Vague" thing. You become increasingly sure of the proposition as the troll chews your arms off in the dark hole you've made for the two of you.

Digested heroes aren't terribly effective. Enjoy your life as troll poop.

Maybe you'll pay a little closer attention next time.

(Go back to 1)

12

An excellent choice. It's what I would have recommended, had you asked. You run up the stairs and find yourself in a cavernous, torchlit room on the third floor of the tower. Every surface in the room, floor to ceiling, is covered in mirrors which are angled in such a way that they point at a melon-sized lens resting on a pedestal in the center of the room. The lens sparkles and hums as it vibrates very slightly on its small velvet cushion; you wonder if it might be magically enchanted in some way. There is only one other doorway in the room, directly across from the entrance and roughly three hundred feet away. The opening leads into a shadowy hallway which you imagine would take you to another set of stairs; you peer into the murky black, but you can't see far enough into the darkness to be sure. You realize, with a pang of gut-wrenching remorse, that you've been eating all of those carrots for nothing.

The lowest torches in the main chamber are too high to reach, even on tippy-toes, and the mirrored walls are too slick to climb. After a bit of additional searching, you notice a demure steel lever between two mirrors on one wall—it looks to operate a network of thin rods and linkages which terminate at regularly spaced mirror panels all around the room. There is a set of darkened glass spectacles hanging on a hook next to the lever and a little slip of parchment stuck to the reflective wall. The note reads:

"Don't change a thing."

You need to be able to see down the hallway to progress. What's the plan, boss?

(continued on next page)

A) This contraption looks like someone took a good deal of care in setting it up, so I don't want to mess with the calibration. I'll just put on the specs and pull the lever. We'll see what happens. (Go to 3)

B) I'll take the lens from the pedestal, then put on the spectacles and pull the lever. (Go to 9)

C) I'm going to break all the mirrors, melodramatically put on the shades, and then pull the lever. (Go to 17)

13

The lift decelerates gently as the indicator on the dial approaches the number "10". The door retracts smoothly to the left, and you see that you have reached your goal: the very top of the spire. You check your equipment, steel yourself for the spectacular duel which is about to take place, and set off.

As you step out of the compartment, the heel of your boot becomes lodged in the gap between the lift and the landing, and your foot slides right out as you continue your stride. You feel the absence immediately and scramble to free the shoe, but the door starts to slide back out of the wall before you're able to wrestle the boot out of the crack. The door closes, barely missing your hand and trapping the already jammed shoe against the frame of the lift. Your panic deepens. You are NOT going to lose these boots before something important gets kicked, and kicked good. Desperate and sensing an impending and irrevocable loss, you take the only action you can think of: you smash the control panel on the wall with the pommel of your sword. Springs and cogs of all shapes and sizes burst out from behind the metal plate, and the lift shakes and shudders to a halt. With the lift's mechanism disengaged, you're able to slide the door back into the wall far enough to wiggle your boot free.

You pull the freshly rescued boot back onto your foot and tighten the laces (on both boots—don't want these babies coming off again). As you stand up again, you realize that you may have just broken your only way back down from the roof. Your anxiety level rises, but then quickly recedes as your eyes catch a sign posted next to the elevator door, which reads:

IN CASE OF FIRE, PLEASE TAKE STAIRS LOCATED
AT SOUTHEAST CORNER OF PANORAMA DECK
TO GROUND LEVEL AND AWAIT FURTHER
INSTRUCTIONS.

SINCERELY,

YOUR FLAMING SPIRE HOSPITALITY TEAM

Well, at least you know there's another way down. It also
looks like everything's been done to code in this place, which
is comforting.

"Can we get started here?" a voice shouts from behind
you. "It's not easy to hold this pose for very long."

You turn around to find The Vague—that cad—with his
hands raised high above his head, fingertips pointing claw-
like in your direction. He has a fiendish sneer on his face and
is staring daggers at you from beneath the hood of his satin
robe. You ask how long he's been standing there.

"The whole time," he replies, biting his lower lip as he
continues to hold his hands all scary.

So he saw the thing with the boot?

He nods, closing his eyes and stifling a laugh.

You look away as you feel a flush rise in your face. After
taking a few deep breaths to re-center yourself, you tell him
in the most heroic voice you can muster that you have trav-
eled far and wide, and that you are here to stop his reign of
terror, once and for all.

"Very well then, we'll just ignore the boot thing and get to
business. Welcome to your end, hero," he says as he drops
his hands from their scary position to cup the luminescent
green gem dangling from a heavy chain around his neck.

"I have the Eye of Greg now, and all the power that comes with it. I'm going to do something really bad, and there's nothing you can do to stop me."

You try to decide what to ask about first: the overly broad threat or the Greg thing. You go with Greg first.

"What?" a visibly surprised The Vague snorts back at you. "You have never heard tell of the great and powerful Greg, the Immortal Crystal Cyclops of the Heddreotic Order?" Your blank stare is answer enough for The Vague, who immediately launches into exposition: "Greg's cyclopean magic was the strongest in the land—it was said that he could summon fire and preserve his own life forever. It is many a hero and many a villain that have been broken on the shores of Greg's mystical island. It's that one, right over there." The Vague points at a group of several islands off the coast to the south. You can't tell which one he means.

Admittedly, The Vague has piqued your interest. You ask how he came to possess such a powerful artifact, especially if Greg was so awesome and was supposed to be immortal.

The Vague's tone drops. "Oh, yeah, I guess you wouldn't know that. You didn't know *him*, so why would you? Greg died a few months back. He had been sick for a really long time, and had been using his power to, you know, heal himself every day, but at one point I think he just got tired of it all and gave up. It was really sad, actually. His wife hasn't been dealing with it very well. I try to stop by when I can to check up on her, her and the kids, but there's only so much you can do, you know? And sometimes you get the feeling they just want to be left alone, so then you're there, and they know you're just trying to be nice, so they don't want to kick you out, but *you* know that you're kind of intruding, so eventually you just make up some excuse to leave, and then they do that polite thing where they protest and tell you not to leave so soon, and then it's awkward all over again." The Vague rubs his left temple absentmindedly. "Anyway, Greg. In his will, he left his Eye," The Vague holds up the gem, "to me. Well, to my master. But then my master gave it to me because he already had something similar, so it's pretty much the same thing as Greg giving it to me. I mean, he probably would have given it directly to me had he known that the boss already had one, but Greg didn't know, and you don't really ask about that kind of thing, so he just had to offer it to my master first. Politics, right? Long story short, I've been working with it for a few weeks, and I can already do some of its spells. It's really started opening up to me, especially in the last few days."

Okay, you're satisfied with the status of the Greg thing. You would say you're sorry you asked, but the situation with Greg's family actually sounds pretty devastating, so you save it. You change topics and ask what The Vague meant earlier, when he said he was going to do something bad.

"Oh, that. Sorry, I completely lost where we were once we started talking about Greg. He's been on my mind a lot lately. Sometimes I'll just lose a whole half hour and then realize I've been standing here staring at his island…" The Vague's attention starts drifting again. You clear your throat, as politely as you're able.

"Yes, the bad thing," says The Vague, coming back to himself. "I'm going to set you on fire. Because you're my nemesis."

You tell him that's a little bland.

"No, I don't mean just *set you on fire*, like in a normal way. It's going to be really impressive and evil—I'm going to use the power of the Eye." He holds the gem up again; it swings back and forth on the chain, and you think you can see a smoky little translucent skeleton swimming around in its depths.

You tell The Vague you're going to have to make it difficult for him—you draw your sword.

"I have no time for such foolishness. Throw down your weapon, hero, or else," The Vague seethes, shaking a fist at you.

You adjust your grip on your sword and ask him why in the world you would want to do such a thing.

"Oh, I don't have to *tell* you why you'll submit, fool—I can *show* you!" The Vague reaches behind a nearby pillar and pulls a small boy into view. The child has ruddy brown hair, cut in a bowl shape, and piercing blue eyes, the whites of which are bloodshot; the tears on the boy's cheeks have not yet dried. "Your emotions make you weak," The Vague taunts. "What say you now, so-called hero?"

You ask whose kid that is.

"Why, he's yours, of course. I captured your son!" The Vague exclaims giddily, the deliciousness of his plot clearly tickling him greatly.

You tell him that the little boy isn't yours.

"What?" The Vague asks, snapping his head to look at the child and then back at you. "Are you sure?"

You tell him you're pretty sure you would know your own son.

"Ah, right. Ummm…" The Vague looks back to the kid, and the three of you stand there silently for a few moments. The Vague breaks the silence again, one hand on the child's shoulder, one hand held up in your direction: "Okay, well, look—you still want to save the kid, right? I mean, you have to, don't you? I thought that was part of your code or creed or something."

You tell him that that's true.

"Okay. Okay, hear me out. Hypothetically speaking, it shouldn't really matter if he's your son or not, because you still have to save him, and I still get to use him as a bargaining chip."

Again, you concede his point.

"Good. Then, if I may, I'd like to propose that we just proceed as planned. Unless you have any objections, of course."

You try to find some gap in his logic, but nothing occurs to you. The boy looks like a nice enough kid, and you *are* sworn to help the innocent. You shrug and agree to play along.

"Great, great. So, I'll be taking your weapons. All of them, please. You can just put them in that receptacle to the right. Yes, that one there." You see him point to a hip-high iron cylinder standing off to your left. The Vague must have meant *his* right. You let it go.

You start to follow his instructions, but a thought gives you pause. What if it's a trick, and he means to kill both you and the child after you've voluntarily disarmed? No, you've got to get the little boy to safety first, you decide. You tell The Vague to send the child over so that you can make sure that he's out of danger; only afterward will you surrender.

"Fine. I suppose you are bound by your code to keep your word, so it doesn't really matter what order we do this in. Here you go," The Vague says as he gives the boy a gentle push behind the shoulders. The child runs to your side and buries his face in your tunic. You give the kid a one-armed hug and then direct your attention back to your enemy. The knave is grinning from ear to ear.

"Now I have you!" screams The Vague, his mystic Greg crystal pulsing and flaring. He chants an incantation as you look down at the child, whose eyes are now glowing green.

The little boy's mouth snaps open, exposing several rows of jagged black teeth. Ho-lee hell. Reflexively, you flinch and let out a short scream as you sap the kid over the head with the handle of your sword. The lights go out in the boy's eyes, and he falls, unconscious, onto a little pile of hay. You're not sure why there's hay up here, but you really don't have time to worry about it now.

The Vague strokes his chin as he considers you. "Very shrewd, hero. I did not think you capable of something so base. It seems I underestimated you."

You protest, saying that it was an accident. A reflex. You would never dream of hurting a child on purpose, and you feel terrible about this.

"Whatever you say, bruiser," The Vague scoffs with a wave of his hand. "It makes no real difference. I'm still going to need those weapons of yours, if you don't mind."

The Eye does its thing again, and every weapon in your possession flies into a floating jumble above your head. The Vague makes a terse hand gesture, and the ball of weapons tumbles over the side of the tower. The villain then returns his focus to you.

"Let's see now," he says, caressing the Eye. "I think I'll be making good on that threat from before."

You ask him which threat he's talking about. He made two.

"The first one," he snaps. "The fire one. Setting you on fire. I'm going to set you on fire now."

The Vague's rising chant echoes throughout the valley. The Eye of Greg pulses and flashes, and a ball of fire forms in the air between The Vague's hands. As you look around wildly for something with which to defend yourself, you realize that you have a pretty low estimation of your chances of surviving this encounter, given the circumstances.

"Die, worm!" The Vague bellows as he releases the fireball, which streaks toward you in a swirl of emerald flame.

Without the aid of your weapons, all that is left to you are your wits (and maybe one or two other items). You face mortal danger, hero. Choose wisely:

A) I don't believe in this scoundrel's parlor tricks. I'm going to call his bluff and charge straight at him. (Go to 4)

B) Let's kill two birds with one stone. I'll use the unconscious demon child as human shield, then run over and beat some ass. (Go to 6)

C) I have pretty strong lungs. I bet I could blow the fireball out and then pummel The Vague with punches—and kicks! (Go to 21)

D) I have a special non-weapon item that I want to use. It's risky, but I think it could work. *You must have the item from the Treasure Room to choose this path* (Go to 22)

14

You press your ear to the door and are greeted by the distinct whir of spinning gears. Suspecting some variety of fatal surprise or another, you quickly pick the lock and, cracking the door just enough to expose the trigger mechanism, disarm the trap. Clever you. You swing the door open and stride over the threshold with your chest puffed out and head held high. Good thing you took your time, huh? The bladed arms of that trap look all slicey.

Your victory celebration will have to wait, however: three brutish guards in the main hall have spotted you and are coming over with all kinds of pointy things to make you go away. You think you might be able to vanquish all three of them with your sword, but it would be a gamble, at best. You check your surroundings for a better option.

For being so big, the room is annoyingly empty. You can't really figure out what the guards were doing in here before you came in, or why they would need to guard a room so spectacularly vacant. Regrettably, you don't have time to puzzle it out now, so you get back to strategizing. You spot a thick rope anchored to the wall on your left—it runs up to a hook in the vaulted ceiling and then back down to a large, candle-laden chandelier. You eyeball it, and you're pretty sure the chandelier hangs directly over the guards' intended path.

The goon squad will be here before long, and you need to make a move, hero. What'll it be?

(continued on next page)

A) They call me the "Monarch of the Jungle". I'm going to grab the rope and swing-kick these fools to the curb. (Go to 19)

B) No point in getting up close and personal with these blockheads. I'll cut the rope and let that chandelier take care of the rest. (Go to 5)

C) These guys look pretty dumb. I bet I could distract them with the "Look Over There" trick and run past them. Let's try that. (Go to 2)

15

The lift stops with a bounce; the dial above the panel indicates the number "8". You gently retrieve your ninja star from the dial and then exit the metal box and read the sign fixed above the door you find in front of you. "Treasure Room", it says. So far, so good.

You open the door and cautiously peer into the room. The place is expansive, but there doesn't seem to be anything resembling treasure in there; there's really not much of anything, save for a gray monolith sitting in the middle of the room and a small window on the wall to your right. The huge boulder has complex, swirled markings all over it which look like they have been carved into the rock and then somehow filled back in, flush, with a slightly lighter gray. The only other thing of note in the room is the distant sound of what you think might be large stones being ground back and forth against each other. Maybe there's a mill or something down in the maintenance department. Like I said, it would have been boring. You think there could be something on the other side of the decorated boulder in the center of the chamber, but you can't see anything from this vantage point. You decide to go in.

The door slams shut behind you as if it were spring-loaded. More disconcerting still is the fact that there is no handle on this side of the door; there is simply a keyhole with a small inscription beneath it. You crouch down to get a better look at the tiny words: *Find Me*. Curious.

Now that you're in here, that grinding sound seems louder and closer than it did before. You think it might be coming from something on the other side of the monolith, so you head in that direction to check things out. As you approach the stone, you can see that it is, in fact, expanding and contracting very slightly in sync with the grinding sound. Well, there you go. The boulder is probably enchanted or something, which is why it has all those markings everywhere. It's making the weird grindy noises all on its own when it changes size. Mystery solved.

You continue on your way across the room, wondering why someone would enchant a rock in such a way. Suddenly, the stone shudders violently and begins to expand and unfold before your eyes. It does not take long for you to realize that this is not a stone at all, but rather a very large and powerful-looking troll, which must have been sleeping prior to your intrusion. Its stone-grind breathing is now much louder in the space, and it has fixed its livid gaze squarely on you. The markings burnt into its skin, which you initially mistook for carvings, lead you to believe that this is a Hypertroll. They're exceedingly rare—you had, up until this point, believed them to be merely the stuff of legend and children's cautionary tales. Through the power of their ancient creators' arcane magic (and the resulting markings: see above), these trolls are rendered impervious to physical attack. People have tried, believe me. Completely invincible to run-of-the-mill violence. They are also surprisingly agile for their titanic size, a fact which this troll is demonstrating by way of its quick approach. Oh! It's also carrying a gigantic club, comprised of three man-sized granite spikes driven through the trunk of a fully intact tree. Sorry, I don't know why I didn't see that before. Thing is huge.

You are fairly sure that your sword is best left sheathed for this encounter: just about everything in here is made of either stone or invincible troll, so you're going to have to figure out a different way to deal with the situation. You look around frantically for some clue as to what your next move should be. The stone floor between the two of you looks a bit weak, as some of the mortar has started to crumble. Above the Hypertroll, several thick wooden rafters are supporting the undoubtedly heavy ceiling. Other than that, there's just, you know, the Hypertroll. Which is starting to get a little too close for comfort.

At the last minute, you remember that you have a special item (you're welcome), which might be of some use to you here.

Do something, quick!

A) Those rafters look promising. I'm going to use my explosive throwing stars on the ceiling. (Go to 10)

B) This thing doesn't look *that* tough. Let's blow it up: I'm going to throw my shurikens directly at the troll. (Go to 16)

C) Let's see if I can make this troll disappear. I'll use the stars on the floor. (Go to 11)

16

You produce the stack of Shinobic ordnance from your left sleeve and assume an authentic assassin's stance. As the Hypertroll begins its final charge, you vault high into the air, scream gibberish at the top of your lungs (you never took the time to learn actual Japanese), and loose your volley of explosive death down at the beast. While you await the *BOOM*, you think about the fact that you couldn't use your sword for this encounter and wonder, seeing as your blade wouldn't have hurt this creature, if the ninja stars are going to successfully injure it, either.

Your query is answered forthwith: the projectiles, instead of penetrating and detonating your foe, bounce off of its thick, magical hide and explode harmlessly in mid-air. Well, not entirely harmlessly: several large pieces of shrapnel lodge themselves painfully into your abdomen and legs as you return to earth. This is, thankfully, hardly noticeable over the troll smashing you into a paste with its gargantuan club.

You are dead. And now, technically a liquid.

You need to read a little more closely, methinks.

(Go to 1)

17

You're sure that you need to pull the lever to proceed, but you're also concerned that this place is likely going to turn into a crucible as soon as you do so. In an effort to limit the amount of reflectivity in the room, you go around and start breaking as many mirrors as you can manage. The ones at ground level are easy enough: you simply apply a bit of percussive force with the pommel of your sword, and Bob's Your Uncle. You then wrap a piece of cloth around your hand, pick up the larger shards, and throw them to break the mirrors which are beyond your reach. The work is repetitive, on account of the room's impressive size and the correspondingly large number of mirrors to be broken, but you've always enjoyed manual labor. You find it quite meditative, actually. You whistle a happy tune of your own composition as you work, and before you know it, the job is done: all of the mirrors are broken. Well, you couldn't quite get the ones mounted to the ceiling, but we can let that slide.

You return to the wall, coolly slide the sunglasses on, and pull the lever, causing an array of hinged panels to swing open all around the room. From behind your shades, you sense the room brighten only marginally; it's definitely not bright enough for you to see if anything is actually happening. It seems the glasses are intended for light much more intense than this and that all you've done is trade one darkness for another. You decide to remove the spectacles, as you're pretty sure that you're no longer in any danger of burning your retinas.

As you evaluate the situation, you can't shake the feeling that you needed all those mirrors to make the lens do whatever it was supposed to do. Now that you've broken them all, there's no way of making this contraption work again. Looks like you're going to have to try to feel your way along the dark hallway. You wolf down a few extra carrots for good measure and head for the doorway.

You stop in your tracks as a horrific wail emanates from the dark and sends shivers down your spine. You hear something slither and scrape along the stone floor beyond your view; the sound quickens as it approaches. You're now rethinking going blindly into the dark space, and you ultimately decide to retreat to the pedestal and see if anything comes out of the tunnel.

What emerges from the hallway a few moments later very nearly causes you to scream. The monster is ethereal vapor, cloaked in a filthy shred of rag and dragging a burning chain along behind it. You recognize it as a Spectral Painbeast, an unspeakable nether-monster which is known to be completely immune to weapons. Swords and stuff, you know. They just pass right through. Apparently one would need to use magic to do any damage at all, and you don't know any. You also remember, with a shiver, that the creatures revel in torturing humans and feeding on their suffering. With an ear-splitting shriek, the Painbeast rushes toward you.

You move to draw your sword, but it's too late (don't beat yourself up, it wouldn't have worked anyway). The Painbeast grasps your head tightly in its smoking claws, bends you over backward, and slithers into your mouth, pulling its burning chain in after it. The links of the chain scorch the inside of your throat and give your terrified screams a strange sizzling, popping quality; with the end of the chain still dangling against your chin, your screaming becomes ever more muffled as your mouth swells shut with blisters. It hurts. A lot. You do note that the smell of your own cooking flesh makes you a little hungry, though. You're not sure if that's weird.

The Painbeast, meanwhile, has taken to devouring you from the inside out. It does this, very slowly and painfully (*Pain*beast, you know), over the course of about three months, somehow keeping you alive for the duration. It's a singularly excruciating experience, and you are relieved beyond words when it's finally over. All that remains of you is your skin, which the Painbeast uses as a human suit.

The creature amuses itself with your husk for some time after your death. It likes to pretend that it's an adventurer, and it does its very best impression of you: it uses your sword to duel its own shadow on the wall, skinsuit jostling as the creature bounces on the balls of its/your feet. It puts on the spectacles and operates the lever with your fumbling hands, flipping the panels in the room open and shut aimlessly for hours on end. Sometimes it just stands somewhere in the middle of the chamber, arms at its sides, swaying slightly and opening and closing your mute lips while the end of its chain flops around like a lolling tongue. And that's how it ends: a lonely monster, standing in an empty room, using a false mouth to mime words that it will never understand.

Yikes. That was rough. I guess someone left that note for a reason, huh?

Let's try again. Fresh start.

(Go back to 1)

18

That sword doesn't belong to you, and you should know better. Is The Vague a scoundrel? Yes. Are you about to have a really important rooftop battle with him which will hopefully end in his capture or death? Absolutely. Does that make it okay for you to start stealing? No. I don't care if all the other adventurers are plundering the dungeons and towers they go capering through, we're talking about you right now. Don't lower yourself to that level. Look at me when I'm talking to you, please. I mean, if you don't stick to your values— LOOK AT ME—if you don't stick to your values, what's the point? I did tell you that you have a perfectly good sword, didn't I? Oh, so you're saying you were going to put the fancy one back afterward? That beggars belief at this point. There was a sign set in stone, for god's sake. Honestly, I'm a little embarrassed for you.

You know, I don't really see the point in helping a grave robber, so I'm going to pack it in early today. I think I need to re-evaluate how I choose my champions.

(You're no hero in my book. Also, that warrior king's ghost cursed you for all eternity, so, yeah. Take a look in the mirror and go back to 1)

19

You free the rope from the wall, toss your head back (hair flowing, teeth glinting), and let loose a jaunty laugh. You yell something heroic and witty as you choke up on the rope and lift your legs into the standard, swinging-hero "L" position. Unfortunately, the ride comes to an end before you've done any of the kicking you'd planned (you're never going to get to use these freakin' boots). It turns out you're quite a bit heavier than the chandelier; you sink back to the floor mid-swing, scraping your butt along the ground for the last yard or so before coming to a halt at the guards' feet. As they descend on you, you decide to initiate Plan B: it's time to hit these dullards with your irresistible charm.

They murder you.

(Go back to 1)

20

Wow. The new boots were really worth that extra dough; the door doesn't stand a chance. Unfortunately, neither do you—the trap behind the door springs before you've even gotten all the way inside, and a number of very eager and very sharp clockwork blades relieve you of your head and most of your other extremities.

Maybe next time a bit more caution would be prudent. At the outset, at least. You're not much good to anyone as a corpse. Or, you know, a pile of corpse pieces.

(Go back to 1)

21

You inhale as deeply as you can and wait for the fireball to come within range. While you wait, you think about the fact that you gave up smoking for this quest and that it's been entirely worth it so far. It's really been paying dividends. Right now, for instance—five years ago, you would never have been able to hold your breath for this long. And all the stairs you've been running in this place? No way, not if you were still smoking. It feels good to be healthy again. Plus, all the money you save!

The moment of truth has come. Just before the fireball makes impact, you blow as hard as you can. The flames snuff out in a little puff of smoke.

You stand there, staring at the now vacant space just in front of your nose. The Vague is also at a loss for words; it seems neither of you had anticipated that something so simple would work. Have any other adventurers ever tried that, you wonder, or are you the first? It seems like there's always some obstacle or monster involving fire on any given quest, but no one seems to try, you know, just *blowing it out*.

The two of you eventually come back to your senses and resume mad-dogging each other. You know it, as does he: this is going to be a battle of attrition. The Vague slings fireball after fireball while you run a zigzag path toward him, using great gulps of air to extinguish each spell in turn. This goes on for a number of minutes, which doesn't sound like very long, but feels like an eternity when you're doing what the two of you are doing. By the time you finally reach The Vague, you're both completely exhausted. Your protracted hyperventilation has left you dizzy and parched, and The Vague's sequential spellcasting has turned him into a sweaty mess—you certainly don't envy him his satin robes at the moment. You wobble over to attack him, but the two of you wind up just leaning on one another like overtaxed pugilists, both starved for oxygen and neither able to make the next move.

Having established that you can't lift your arms, you think that you should probably do something to further your current endeavor. A psych-up seems in order, so you try to spur yourself with righteous indignation at The Vague's crimes against humanity. You can't think of a single one. I mean, you know he's generally a *bad guy*, but for some reason you can't think of anything he's done in particular, at least nothing which you could ascribe to him with certainty. You realize that he always threatens to do evil deeds in a very broad way, and that bad things wind up happening around the time he mentioned, but you're never quite sure that it was he who actually committed the deed.

That's when it hits you: the vagueness. Even though you can't remember any of his literal crimes, you sure as hell can remember a lot of the figurative ones. There have been dozens of times when you showed up at the wrong place for a duel with this guy because he gave you nebulous directions. A laundry list of other time-wasting transgressions tumbles through your mind, and the anger over every euphemism, double entendre and ambiguity to which this monster has subjected you over the years is suddenly made manifest in a flurry of blows, which you rain down on your weakened foe. You're back in the game. Each of your punches finds its target and exacts its price, but it turns out that The Vague is frustratingly good at dodging your kicks, even in his diminished state: not one of your foot-based attacks has connected. You're not even sure why you bought these boots anymore.

Just as you're about to let the final blow fall from on high, The Vague grasps the Eye of Greg and barks a short, desperate incantation. A crackling sphere of energy emanates from the gem and expands violently, knocking you off balance and causing you to stumble backward. You regain your feet just in time to see the light in Greg's Eye go out; the crystal has cracked under the strain and is now leaking tendrils of opalescent green smoke up into the mountain air. The smoky little skeleton which you had seen in the crystal earlier has also drifted free of its confines. You watch as it extends a yearning hand toward The Vague—who doesn't notice—before it is snatched away by a gust of wind and scattered into nothingness.

Your nemesis is stumbling around precariously close to the drop-off and staring up at the darkened Eye, held aloft. You decide to seize the opportunity: finally, it's Kickin' Time. You take a running start and jump higher than you ever have before, spinning as you leave the ground. You are a force of nature, and your incipient hurricane kick is aimed squarely at The Vague's stupid head. This is going to be awesome. He's going to fly so far.

"My master has forsaken me," The Vague says in a broken tone as his forlorn gaze finally leaves the ruined gem in his hand. He whirls around to hurl the Eye from the spire, but he doesn't realize how close he is to the edge. Your quarry steps into space and plummets over the side of the tower, leaving your wicked awesome kick connecting with nothing but empty air.

You shout an expletive and catch your balance just before you would have followed the villain to your doom. After taking a deep breath (the boots will have their day—*patience*), you straighten your tunic, fix your hair, and shuffle over to the edge to watch your enemy fall the rest of the way down. You think you see him hit the ground—he stops getting smaller, anyhow—but the impact doesn't make a sound.

Well, shucks. That was kind of anticlimactic. You look around to see if anyone can give you some indication of what you're supposed to do now. Over on the stack of hay, the little boy is coming around and seems to be free of The Vague's influence. Otherwise, crickets. You see if you can glean any info from the last few things The Vague said before he died, about his master and stuff. It was all pretty cryptic, right? Leave it to that guy to keep you guessing.

You're not sure who this master of his is, nor are you confident that you should be starting fresh beef with someone you don't even know. Besides, you've probably earned a little R&R, right? Then again, you *are* supposed to be all valiant and heroic and everything, and it would probably just nag at you the whole time if you were to go home and try to ignore it. You'd also get another chance to use the boots properly, which you're actually still pretty frustrated about. You know you said you'd be patient, and you're trying to keep your cool, but you're having a really hard time dealing with it at this precise moment. Crap—you just remembered that you have to walk back down all those stairs. Oh, and you have to find this kid's parents! *Great.*

A beetle scuttles past your left foot and stops near the brink. You gaze down at the bug's shiny black carapace and watch as its thick, segmented antennae twitch around to test a reddish pebble sitting in front of it. You sigh through your nose, take a short step forward, and kick the beetle off the tower. The insect sails off in a shallow arc before opening its wings and flying away.

Doesn't count.

Hey, friend? Buddy? Yeah, hi. Any idea what do you want to do now?

A) I got the bad guy I was after, and I'm pretty exhausted, so...yeah. I'm out. Bye. (You're done. Close the book, quitter.)

B) There is a villain at large, and a hero's work is never done. I must continue my quest. (Go to 24)

22

You pull your filigreed mirror from your pack and, grasping the handle tightly with both hands, stare down the coming inferno. The Vague's fire spell gathers speed as it approaches; you aim the mirror's reflective surface back at your nemesis and brace for impact.

You stare dumbly at the molten remains of your fancy new mirror as the Vague's spell vaporizes the better part of your torso. Right through. I mean, it didn't even slow down. As you no longer have a contiguous spinal cord, you're finding it exceedingly difficult to remain upright; you fall where you stand. You hear The Vague's high-pitched cackle draw nearer as your vision begins to fade. Your fate is sealed.

We did establish that it was a normal mirror, right? I mean, we were both there when you were trying to get it to wake up or grant you wishes or whatever it was you were trying to do. I'm not sure what you thought was going to happen here. Did you see that gnarly fireball he shot at you? That thing was crazy.

Sorry things didn't work out. You almost had him.
This close.

(Go back to 1)

23

I like you. You've got balls. Figuratively speaking. Whatever, poor choice of words. In any case, you're absolutely right about the gender thing—just keep the righteous indignation to a minimum at parties, friend. It gets old. Still, you've got integrity, which might just help you on this quest. Take this set of sweet explosive ninja stars for your trouble—they're sure to come in handy later.

(Go to 1)

24

You must continue your quest, huh? Then you must...sit, unfortunately. And wait. For the next book to come out. You know, so you can continue your journey. Quest, whatever. I admire your pluck, by the way—not everyone would persevere the way you have. No, I'm not trying to change the subject. I'll have it done soon. Soon, I don't know! These things take time. Look, I'm working on it as fast as I can, okay? Geez.

THE END. SO FAR.

(Nice work, hero.)

Notes

Notes

Notes

Notes

Notes

The world needed more stories.
The following people did something about it:

Ale$$andra
Corryn Anderson
Matthew Barnard
Sonja Bonja
Amanda Brasher
Tim Butler
Jennifer Campney
Paul & Ann Cartwright
Chelsey
Donna Coon
Glenn Copeland
Robert Cornejo
Rani Covington
Jennifer Crocker
Mike Danylchuk
Kathleen Dirks
Mary K. English
Ian Fincham
Tiffany Fox
Frieda
Andrew "Wayward Backer" Foster
Tiago Fumian
Torii Gardiner
Christine Gengaro
Shelly Gibbons
George Gibbs
Gilbert
Jon & Heather Greening
Jim Hardison
Neal "What Would Picard Do" Harris
Jonathan & Amber Hartje
Cristin Hipke
Shannon Hong
Peter Irvine
Joanna
Simon Karlsson
Diana Y. Lee
Dan Lowry
Lisa Lowry

Peter Lowry
Tom & Colleen Lowry
Donald "Skeet" Matson
Niall McMahon
Kitty Milar
Patti & Bob Murray
Jeff Narucki
Christopher P. Nash
Kostas & Nicole Niktas
J.H. Nofziger
Alvaro Ortiz
Bob & Victoria Patton
Jessica Patton
Torrie Patton
Chuck Pickelhaupt
Poodle Lover
Carolyn Reid
Dan Rhodes
Ringo
Emily Robinson
Bastian Roeder
Benedict Roeser
Sarah
Bethany Scherbarth
John Singletary
Anthony Snow
Luke Storry
Melisse Sullivan
Tina and Tim
Thorin "T$" Tobiassen
Michael Tramov
Zach Urbina
Chris & Tracey Vendilli
Rebecca Vogel
Jeremy Voss
Carl Whitaker
Forrest & Kathryn Whitaker
Seth W. Whitaker
The Whitaker Boyer Family
Aaron Zeller

About the Author

Insofar as anything can be said with certainty about someone's identity, Rhett W. Whitaker is the person who wrote this book. His repeated claims of living in Berlin, being a proud husband and father, and having a few more books in the works could not be independently verified.